TEN

MILES

ONE

WAY

Also by Patrick Downes

Fell of Dark

TEN MILES ONE WAY

PATRICK DOWNES

PHILOMEL BOOKS

This work was completed with the help of a 2015
Creation Grant from the Vermont Arts Council
and the National Endowment for the Arts.

PHILOMEL BOOKS

an imprint of Penguin Random House LLC
375 Hudson Street, New York, NY 10014

Library of Congress Cataloging-in-Publication Data
Names: Downes, Patrick, 1968– author. | Title: Ten miles one way / Patrick
Downes. | Description: New York, NY : Philomel Books, [2017] | Summary:
In the wake of a near-fatal car accident, Isaac Kew, twenty, recalls a very long
walk he took three years earlier with his bipolar girlfriend, Nest. | Identifiers:
LCCN 2015041653 | ISBN 9780399544996 | Subjects: | CYAC:
Manic-depressive illness—Fiction. | Mental illness—Fiction. | Love—Fiction. |
Automobile accidents—Fiction. | Classification: LCC PZ7.1.D687 Ten 2017 |
DDC [Fic]—dc23 | LC record available at https://lccn.loc.gov/2015041653

Printed in the United States of America.   ISBN 9780399544996
1 3 5 7 9 10 8 6 4 2

Edited by Jill Santopolo.   Design by Semadar Megged.
Text set in 10.5-point Garth Graphic Std.

In the Age of Gold,

Free from winter's cold,

Youth and maiden bright

To the holy light,

Naked in the sunny beams delight.

—William Blake

Her *pleasure* in the walk must arise from the
exercise and the day.

—Jane Austen

THE WHY

It's been five days since Nest drove a car into a tree at sixty miles an hour. She's sleeping. Unconscious, at any rate. If and when she wakes, she will face questions. What else?

I was there in the car, next to her, a helpless passenger. What do I remember about the collision? Not much. My own memory of it can't be trusted. I remember—.

I remember the Chimaera behind the wheel.

The Chimaera roaring in the middle of a great fire. The lion roaring fire. The goat bleating. The poised snake. No one can get near, it's all so hot.

I've been questioned by doctors and the police. I don't mention the Chimaera. Otherwise, I'm honest.

"Nest asked me if I wanted to go for a drive, and I said yes."

"I remember my life up until I shut the passenger door."

"I don't know why Nest drove the car into a tree. I don't think she intended to."

"Yes, I know she's totaled two cars in two years. But—. You don't know about her headaches. The first time, a headache shut her eyes. The same thing happened to her father."

"I've known Nest almost half my life. Her boyfriend, yes, off and on. Off, lately."

"Suicide? I don't think that's in her. She gets—. Her mind. She's bipolar, sometimes psychotic. Yes. No. She seemed happy and calm enough when we started, then BOOM."

"I'd say black ice. Maybe, snow. It's December, right?"

"No drugs, no alcohol. You must know that already."

"Boom. Just boom."

"I'm alive."

"My name is Isaac Kew."

■ ■ ■

Nest calls me Q. I am, right now, an empty Q. Q without Nest.

I fell in love with Nest in eighth grade, when we were thirteen, at exactly the same moment when I hated her. She cast me as a fire hydrant in a class play she'd written. She has, since we met, teased me for being stupid, but that's only because she told me first thing she had a silent P in front of her name, and I believed her. I was gullible. But I was gullible because I had no reason to doubt the first girl I'd decided was beautiful.

"P-N-E-S-T," I said, spelling it out. "But silent. Like the P in pneumatic. Or pneumonia."

"That's right," Nest said. "Just like that."

"Cool," I said.

Then she said: "I think you'd make a great fire hydrant."

Every so often, Nest relents. Five days ago, the night of the collision—I remember this—Nest said, "You've always had a giant love for me, Q. It's not stupid to love. But my brain makes love seem ridiculous. I am the Chimaera. Beast and girl, and deadly. I am unlovable."

That last sentence: "I am unlovable." That would have been enough for the police to think Nest really had wanted to die outright, commit suicide, and was willing to take me with her.

I'm not convinced.

I believe, no matter how Nest's illness rips her up, Nest

knows I love her. Nest knows her mother and father love her. It's difficult to end your life when you know you're loved. Not impossible. But difficult.

Nest was right, though. I don't have her intelligence—or trouble. I'll never be forced to take a drug to calm down. I'll never see the inside of a mental ward, except to visit. And I'll never have a mythical beast living inside of me.

■ ■ ■

I've been writing almost five days straight to no one in particular. To the you we all have inside of us, not ourselves but no one else either. Not quite a god or a devil; not quite a friend; not quite a hero. No one in particular, but someone just the same.

There are two styles of handwriting here. Myself in one. Most of it, though, in a handwriting to show when Nest's speaking aloud to me. Speaking and speaking for miles.

Three years ago, when we were seventeen, Nest asked me to go on a walk with her. I'm writing out half of it, ten miles. This is in case she dies. I don't want the world to think she died without ever having been loved.

■ ■ ■

Nest had never asked me on one of her walks before. Manic walks, when she thought and felt in a rush and talked to herself and somehow made it home alive. She always went alone, once a week, sometimes more, for months, depending on how she slept. She's someone for whom sleep was a disaster. It was her father who started taking her on walks, day or night, when she was young. I knew that, but not—.

I don't want to say too much too soon. I want you to hear what happened over the course of a long walk, or half a long walk. The second half doesn't matter. I don't know if the second half even exists. I don't remember ever making it home.

MILE ONE

We could see our breath at the beginning.

Nest buttoned her flannel. It might have been her father's originally, I don't know. She swam in it. I remember an elbow patch, the Nepalese flag, for no reason I could guess. Nest isn't Nepalese. A mystery. And another mystery: a raised scar of blue thread above the chest pocket. Knife, match, bullet, age? She wore the red flannel over some kind of white camisole or T-shirt. I couldn't really tell. You don't need to be sure of anything to love a girl.

"Where are we going?"

There was only one rule, and I broke it almost immediately. I shouldn't have talked.

"Are we headed somewhere specific?"

Silence.

"Nest?"

"Don't say anything," she said. "You promised you wouldn't say anything. It hasn't even been five minutes."

■ ■ ■

No, don't apologize. I said you could go with me, the whole way, if you didn't say anything. Not *I'm thirsty,* not *I'm hungry,* not *I'm tired and my feet hurt.* Definitely not *Where are we going?* The whole adventure, Q—wandering, drifting this way and that, north by northeast by southwest, mood and question and whim and hunger and thirst and.

You're not allowed to comment either. Nothing.

A silent companion. That's what you are. Like a coin in my pocket. Or my own heart. Or, you know, my spleen, my gall bladder—.

Pretend you're a penny, or a rib, or my tiny heart.

■ ■ ■

You haven't done anything like this before, I promise. You walk all the time: school, coffee, diner, pizza, here, there. The neighborhood. But you've never walked like this, Q. Never so far, and never with me. Never for me.

When I walk alone, at the start, I'm barely touching ground. I'm skimming. Levitating a little. But the farther I walk, the heavier I get. The ground gets closer bit by bit. At some point I realize I've landed. Sole on concrete.

Somewhere along the loop that begins with my parents' house, I run into myself. I can't explain it any other way. It sounds nuts. There I am, loitering, waiting for me to arrive. It's happened all over. Stairways, pews, public bathrooms, trees, stoops, the library stacks. Alleys, windows, mirrors. Once, I was steam coming through a manhole cover. Last month, I could've sworn I was the cap on a doorman's head. I'm serious. I wasn't, though. I was his shoe.

Kidding. I was, actually, the doorman—.

By the end of the walk, I'm sleep. Get me to bed.

■ ■ ■

A walk like this: what can I compare it to so you'll understand?

You've fished a million times. I went with you and

your uncle that once. I remember all the ropes, rods, and buckets; and the salt and seagulls and.

Walking and fishing start the same way. You gauge the sky and take your best guess: weather or no weather? Then you cast off. For a little distance, you can look over your shoulder at the docks, the piers, the other boats, everything you recognize. The wake stretches all the way home. You're still home.

Forget the wake: it's the going out that matters. You motor out, *churr, churr, churr.* You're on the compass.

I love going forward, the slow forward, in any direction. Not even very far. All of a sudden—whoops. The whole world drops off. Home's gone. You're in the ocean now. At sea. Everything that surrounds you goes much deeper than you know.

Our neighborhood, Q, no matter how well we think we know it, is an ocean. We don't know anything. We know what the houses and buildings look like, but we don't know what goes on in any of them, not really. We've grown up our whole lives right here, in the city, seventeen years: it's completely familiar and totally unknown. Every block is like the ocean, pure muscle, but concrete, not water. All the street has to do is flex, even a little, and we might flip over and drown in pavement. Swallowed up. Crushed—.

Cobblestones.

That's a great word: *cobblestones.*

I'm not trying to make you afraid. Home is behind us, out of sight, but everything's okay. We're shipshape and right side up. We're chugging along. The weather's fine. No storms, no big waves. No sharks. No danger at all. I love the ocean, and I love the city.

We're going for a walk. The city is beautiful even when it's not.

Trust me.

■ ■ ■

We'd barely gone five blocks, and I already had a slight fever. I felt a little trippy. Whatever was solid, even my own body, seemed to liquefy. I thought, This is what it means to be around a person who's not quite in her right mind.

This is the honest truth. To walk with Nest when she felt manic—that's the right word, manic, *a word I didn't know then but know now—was to walk with a girl whose own mind was a fever.*

I trusted her, though. I trusted her the way I would trust a river.

Nest flows one way, undisturbed until disturbed, constant

but wandering, and entirely natural. I knew she was swim-
mable, but I'd had to wait. I'd had to wait for her to invite
me. I'd waited and waited. For years, really, I'd waited, from
thirteen to seventeen. We were friends, off and on, we would
sometimes talk, and we'd done this and that together, like go
fishing once, and one time ice-skating, but I could never find
the right way to get any nearer.

Finally, the river spoke to me. She called me at six in the
morning, October 4, and told me to come.

I trusted Nest. That's what matters.

■ ■ ■

I didn't sleep last night. Not that I remember anyway. I
might have dozed, but.

If I count it up right now, I've averaged about two and
a half hours of sleep a night for four nights, so ten hours
in four days. That's why I haven't gone to school in a
week. I'm useless. Three nights ago, I slept for a blissful
five hours straight, but only about two hours the next
night and almost nothing last night. I'm so tired; I have
that queasy feeling, sick. And I can't really trust my eyes.
My eyeliner is fire. I had to look twice at your shoes because I was wondering about the pink. They're not, but

for a second or two they were PINK. Sounds are coming to me from far away, from the end of a long empty hall. Everything echoes.

■ ■ ■

I'm not sleeping because I'm not sleeping. My mind: up and down, round and round, always. My mood. You know how it is. I'm afraid to sleep. The constant dreams and terrors. Sometimes I fall straight into dreams. It's like.

Falling from an airplane.

Sitting there, looking out of the window seat. Such empty sky. Nothing but cold, blue light. I don't want to close my eyes, but the sun, Q: it's bright. It just won't stop, ever. It might blind me to sleep. I don't want to sleep, though. I want to stay awake. I lean into the window and look down. I imagine myself outside the plane, strapped into seat 17A, hovering six miles above the earth, above the clouds, almost past oxygen. I'm fighting to keep conscious in the thin air and bright light. A never-ending faint, a constant falling.

How long do you think it would take to fall six miles?

I want to land, go home, see you, ride my bike to school: life. But falling, or wanting to fall, seems stronger, so much stronger than needing to get home. I don't have wings. So I fall, mile after mile, through all the fists of clouds.

Dreams.

Sometimes I fall through them, on and on, until I hit the ground at a thousand miles an hour. I never understand why I don't explode the exact moment I wake up. Bones and goop every which way.

▪ ▪ ▪

Do you think a plane can die midair and go down, *fwoop*, like a bird shot to death? All the people, two hundred passengers and crew, terrified, made to die together and alone. What about the people who won't cry or pray? Like that guy who's pretty sure his wife is having an affair, would he strangle her? Or that woman with her baby, would she breastfeed or smother him? Will that couple kiss or hug or—? While the man behind them sleeps all the way to the bottom of the sky.

Touch the window, Q. Go ahead. Feel the whole plane trembling?

The plane's a gigantic steel husk, heavier than air, working to break itself and scatter its load of human seeds over the earth. A few seconds before the crash, what would I do? Would I scratch my face, tear my hair out, forget everybody I ever knew? You'll be a promise I get when I die, when the plane hits the ground. So fast.

Phew.

My mind, I know, but.

I'm making all this up. I've never even been on a plane.

I imagine the plane filled with a noiseless noise—. A hum, deep and gentle. It might even be coming from inside me. It might be the sound of the engine of my imagination.

▪ ▪ ▪

Five after seven. The traffic is just waking up. We could still walk in the street without getting killed. A different story an hour from now. An hour from now, we'll be at the bridge. Up the arch and down the arch: a mile, outside to core. The whole thing, cables and concrete and iron towers, vibrating and coughing and, and clattering.

It's a little cool. Not uncomfortable, though. It's barely October, only a few days in, so that warm, coppery feeling will catch up to us any second. We're walking, and the fog's almost gone. Almost time to take the flannel off.

■ ■ ■

My psychiatrist until very recently, Elaine Ruff—. Wait. Did I already tell you this—?

That's a terrible way to start a story. You should always start a story with something memorable. Also, you should know your audience, like, for instance, if you've told the story before to the same person. Especially true when you're talking to an audience who may be afraid of what they've gotten themselves into by agreeing to walk with a madwoman.

Let me start again.

My psychiatrist until very recently, Elaine Ruff, looks like a beagle—.

This is just getting worse. Always start a story with a true sentence. Dr. Ruff looks nothing at all like a beagle. Except for her ears.

I'm exaggerating. Dr. Ruff's a liar, but she's a very pretty woman.

Especially if you like beagles.

I'm going to shut up a minute, but when I start again—. I'll start at the next stop sign.

■ ■ ■

She's someone for whom sleep is a disaster.

Remember that sentence. I even give you permission to use it. You might think the person who said it was really smart, maybe even a poet. My psychiatrist until very recently, Elaine Ruff, said it. She's not that smart, definitely not a poet. She's not even kind or insightful, but she said it. She was telling the truth, we know that much.

She was talking to my parents. The four of us were in her office. She had a broken window in one wall, all tape and cardboard. The window I'd smashed the day before, when I kicked it out.

■ ■ ■

She dared me. I said, "I'm angry. I'm so angry. I could knock a hole in a wall or punch a window."

"Oh?" she said. She looked at me a long time. Her nose is a knife. "That's pretty angry."

I just looked at her: "—"

"Would you knock a hole in my wall or punch out one of these windows?"

"Yes," I said, "but I'd get in trouble."

"No, no," she said. "Go ahead."

"?"

"You're that angry, go ahead. I can fix a hole, replace a window."

"You'd fix it yourself, or someone you'd hire?"

"I'd pay someone."

"You take money to fix people's brains, to work on something no one really understands, the miraculous human mind. You probably write enough prescriptions to get a cramp in your hand. How many—? But when you need to do something, something practical, you have to hire someone."

"You're angry."

"I said that."

"And I'm included," she said. "You're angry with me. Go ahead, break a window."

"I won't get in trouble?"

"Of course not." Her knife nose and needle eyes. "I'm encouraging it. Please."

For a moment I thought, *I'm about to do something stupid.* But I was angry, and I wanted to let it all go, and.

I stood up, walked across the room, and kicked out her window, a sort of judo kick. I don't know judo, but I screamed when I kicked. A warrior scream. The window shattered and crashed and tinkled into the alley and on the floor. Glass fangs in the mouth of the window frame.

For a little while I balanced on one foot, my other foot midair. Not a sound.

I walked back to my comfortable armchair.

Ruff sat very still. She cleared her throat, a beagle bark. Then, she let me have it: "You'll repay me for the cost of that repair."

I'm like: "!"

I couldn't say anything. I just stared at her in total—. I couldn't believe it.

"Every cent." Her lips didn't move at all. "Or your parents will."

"!"

"You have to leave now. The next time I see you—"

"You challenged me." I yelled it. I felt like I'd suddenly woken up. "You said, 'I'm encouraging it. Go ahead.' You said, 'Please.' Why should I, or my parents, pay for your stupidity? You didn't think I'd do it? You didn't think I'd have the courage to kick out your window? Did you think I'd be afraid of you? That I'm not angry enough? You underestimated me. Or overestimated yourself. Both, probably."

Ruff stood and pointed to her door. "Leave. I'll call your parents immediately."

"You're a disgrace to your profession." That's what I said

on my way out. "A disgrace. And I should know. You're number six in this parade. Six in two years. I thought the one who didn't wear pants—Dandelion, Dinderlinn, whatever—. That pervert tried to hide the fact he didn't wear pants by sitting behind a big desk. One day, someone in the office next door started screaming like she was being stabbed or set on fire, screaming and shrieking, and Dinderlinn jumped up. Startled. Then I was startled. A fifty-year-old man: waist-long beard, bug eyes, and flagpole skinny. Jacket, shirt, tie, and blue-and-white-striped boxers. His little you-know-what trying to break out. But no, you're the worst. You're a snake."

"Leave."

"And what if I'd broken my foot? Or cut myself on the glass and bled to death on the rug? A rug I hate, since it clashes with the paint. It hurts my eyes being here. Gives me a headache."

"Leave."

"I'm going."

▪ ▪ ▪

"I know you don't like the medications." Dr. Ruff again, talking with my parents the next day. "And I admit, the track record with Nest leaves a great deal to be desired. Mistakes, yes."

We sat there, all three of us, Mom, Dad, me, with our arms crossed. Three judges waiting for the guilty to stop talking, to be quiet, so we could argue among ourselves: exile or firing squad?

"But medication is a reasonable approach. Otherwise," she was finishing up, "your daughter will become a lost girl."

"A lost girl." My mother smiled at that. Not a happy smile, and you know her voice, mild as milk. "Did you give Nest the impression she could break the window or do damage without—?"

"I did."

"But then you changed your mind? What if she—?"

"I want to know what you mean by a lost girl." My father hadn't spoken a word until then. He has a voice like a grizzly bear, right? Nothing like milk. And he has those eyebrows, that frown. He's scared you enough times, like he's deciding whether or not to tear your head off. There's no one kinder than my dad. It's extremely funny that he lets people go around thinking he's an assassin or bodyguard.

He rubbed my mother's shoulder. "Sorry for interrupting you."

Dr. Ruff had stopped dead when my father spoke. Instinctively, she put her hand on her desk phone, like she wanted to call for help. The zoo, I guess, or a game warden. I could see her thinking, *How'd this animal get into my office?*

"A lost girl?" My father frowned. "Explain this, please."

Dr. Ruff smoothed her hair and let out her doggy cough. "I meant only that Nest's welfare matters, and, at this rate, if she's not medicated—." She tried out a smile, which might charm men but not bears. My father waited. "It's my belief she needs to be medicated. Your reluctance I understand. But Nest needs to sleep. She needs to sleep when she gets. Unwell. The sleeplessness only worsens her overall health. Her judgment suffers. Look—."

A bird, something between a vulture and a hummingbird, burst out of the wall. Outside, from under the broken window. It must have been huddling there, a hole in the brick, listening in, shaking as birds do, until it had had enough.

"I'm not the right therapist for your daughter." Dr. Ruff folded her hands in her lap. "I'm not. I realized this the moment I heard myself challenge her. I put us both in danger. And when Nest stood up, I don't have to tell you—"

"Dr. Ruff." My father leaned forward in his chair.

"Mr. Fitzgerald, I'm angry with myself."

"When I think of a lost girl, Dr. Ruff, I think of a girl who might die in the street from a drug overdose. I think of a girl who might commit suicide or become a prostitute. A girl who runs away from home to find someplace better, never to be seen again by her family. Maybe it doesn't have to be so dramatic. Maybe a lost girl is a girl who doesn't succeed. A girl who seems to have everything going for her but falters in her task of happiness or fails to get enough sleep. I'm not sure what you mean. I know this: we know our daughter. I, we, will not lose Nest. She struggles in school. She's way too—like her mother—way too smart. She walks long distances to settle her mind. She will not, however, disappear, like a watermelon seed down the kitchen drain."

Dr. Ruff coughed and ran her fingers through her hair. My mom dropped her head. As for me, I started crying.

My father reached into his jacket pocket for his checkbook and a pen. "Now." He flipped to the first blank check, #5009. "While I find yesterday's misunderstanding an indictment of your own sense, and I'm more than half tempted to lodge a formal complaint, I'll write this check to cover the cost of the window."

My mother gripped my hand, and my father held the door. We didn't look back.

Dr. Ruff in the rearview. Gone.

"Why is Nest crying?" My father must have been asking my mother or himself or the sidewalk. Not me. Definitely not me.

My dad, Q, my dad hasn't spoken to me, really spoken to me, in so long, and he. He doesn't know, right? Not for sure. How could I tell him I was crying because he might be totally wrong? I might be lost already.

■ ■ ■

Watch. You nearly stepped—.

Poor mouse.

Oh, see that? It twitched. It's alive. Only a cat would do this. Savages. Look at its tiny eye. I swear this mouse knows it's about to die. It's capable of feeling sad, lonely. Honestly, can't you see it asking itself, *Why me?* This mouse is a philosopher mouse. *The universe is chaotic,* it's thinking, *meaningless, and there's no god for us mice.* It shuddered because the whole freezing universe, totally blind to mice, landed right on top of it, *whoosh*. Maybe not, but that's an eye with intelligence. I know it. That mouse is pure brain.

Brain and whiskers.

And it's lying in the sun. A long, golden beam from heaven about to lift it away.

Do you want to put it out of its misery—?

You want to? A tiny bit or a lot?

I've done it before. I hate the suffering. It's awful, though, killing, even for mercy. Your foot never forgets the body, the resistance, if you've crushed something, and you never look at a shovel the same way again. This is close killing, intimate, and it's really tiring. I can't do it this time. I don't have the energy or heart. I haven't slept enough. Sometimes mercy asks too much, or costs—.

Come on. You don't have to. It's something I do, or not. We'll walk and walk, for hours, but I can't kill this mouse. It's too exhausting.

■ ■ ■

I knew I would kill the mouse for Nest.

People question love that comes quick and goes deep, as if it couldn't be meaningful, long lasting, or true. But if a woman can be struck and killed in the street by a tire that peels off

a semi, or a man can find himself permanently paralyzed in
a moment by a stroke, or some child gets hit by lightning,
survives, and wears the long, feathery scar forever—sudden,
powerful events with everlasting consequences—why should
love that arrives from nowhere, at any age, even thirteen,
and changes everything, seem any less possible or true? And
doesn't this quick and deep and true love expect a person to
do whatever is reasonably possible for the sake of the beloved?

I would walk with Nest as far as she wanted to go, maybe
around the world. So why wouldn't I kill this mouse to save it
from pain? Why wouldn't I relieve Nest?

■ ■ ■

You didn't have to do that, Q. I know it's terrible. I'm
sorry. You're a gentle soul.

Say a prayer with me. I always say a prayer over dead
animals, dead anything. Snakes, squirrels, birds, spiders,
moths. I even blessed a cat once. Squashed in the street.
I buried that one myself.

I have to bless them all. Like this mouse. A few seconds of silence, okay?

Go.

MILE TWO

"Where there is vegetation the law of Nature has decreed that there shall be rabbits; where there are rabbits, Providence has ordained there shall be dogs."

That's a quote from—.

I'll tell you later. It just popped into my head. I don't have any kind of order for what I'm saying. There's no script. I'm.

Hungry.

Where are we? Where can we eat around here?

Oh my. A couple blocks over: Geno's. You can get a

morning cannoli. You like cannoli? I want a limoncello muffin. Maybe two. And some kind of meat.

■ ■ ■

There's nothing to show for last night, all the time not sleeping. I finished up plans for a chicken coop my parents won't let me build. I can't blame them. It has electronic surveillance, motion sensors, and automatic doors. Egg chutes, of course. It would cost, I don't know, a lot. Not to mention we can't even legally raise chickens—unless we can. There must be some kind of poultry law or everybody would have chickens. Wouldn't you keep chickens if you could—?

I don't know why I thought about a coop.

Sometime overnight I took ten thousand photographs of two dead ladybugs upside down on the windowsill and a cobweb. Very arty. And I played one bass chord as long as possible—*duhh-dummdumm, duhh-dummdumm*—before my hand cramped up. Forty-nine minutes straight. Good, right? I'd estimated forty-five, but hoped for an hour.

I've mostly been reading, though. Reading like a fiend. Do fiends read? Probably not, busy as they are with their bloodlust. I'm gobbling words and pages. This makes up for some of the phases when I couldn't read at all—like swimming through a sea of bricks. I think I've started six books and finished four others in a week. And the essays and blogs and poetry and.

I watched an episode of *The Mary Tyler Moore Show* from 1975, "Chuckles Bites the Dust." It's considered one of the best sitcom episodes ever, according to some guy on *Huffington*. I'd never heard of it, the episode. The show, yes, because my parents went through a seventies binge a year ago. *Mary Tyler Moore, MASH, Carol Burnett.* God, Chuckles the clown. Really good, really smart. I thought so, at least. YouTube it.

■ ■ ■

I feel another quote coming on.

Perfection, Q. How do we make anything perfect? Do we have to add and add to it until we can't anymore? Or do we get closer to perfection when we take away all we can, strip a thing down to its bare essentials, its simplest lines? To the French author Saint-Exupéry—the man who wrote *The Little Prince*—perfection comes only when you have everything taken away. I agree with him. But not just about things; people, too. Think about it. Eyeliner: I add it, but it takes me farther from perfection, not closer. Same with lip gloss, and, I guess, clothes. Perfection should be my naked body. Who says it isn't? When I am naked, I am Nest, exactly Nest. I'm seventeen, and I'll never be seventeen again. Simple perfection, raw perfection—.

Saint-Exupéry was a pilot, and his book *Wind, Sand and Stars*, my current favorite book of all time, is all about planes and flight and survival and adventure and. It's beautiful. In that book, when Saint-Exupéry talks about perfection of craft, he's talking about the fuselage of a plane, but he could be talking about a painting or a faucet or the human body, maybe even a thought, a story, or.

Love.

Love is perfect when it's simple and undecorated. No words, only the expression in someone's eye, her touch, his kiss. "I love you" is a simple sentence, pretty clear, unless your idea of love crashes up against the other person's idea of love. Then you've got a problem—.

I wish I could be naked. I want to be raw.

■ ■ ■

I shouldn't have said *raw*. Raw makes me think of meat. Meat makes me think of blood. Blood leads me back to my dreams.

I dream about blood. Blood and hunting. I hunt, I'm hunted. I run and run and murder and escape murder, barely. Last week, one night, I slept so well all the way up until a storm of stones tore through the sky. The stones came in bursts, like.

A giant throwing rocks, fistfuls of them. Little kids falling down at a playground, their mothers and fathers, their brothers and sisters and dogs, dying. An ocean of stones. I woke up when a woman—I think she's from the neighborhood, a bank teller—when she fell. Her skull was opened up, broken by a stone. She was blood. She tripped over her dream child and crushed him.

I woke up sick. I wanted to throw up. But then I fell right back to sleep and into the next dream. A faceless woman singing to me while she cut my fingernails. At first, I didn't let her near me. Once, when I was five, my mother was scared by a car horn, and she cut into my finger with a pair of scissors. See the scar? I bled all over and cried. So the woman in the dream hummed to calm me down until I opened my hand. She used a pair of small scissors with curved blades. I'll forever remember the scissors. And the texture of her skin: cornmeal, or caked with dirt. She might have been a corpse. A dead woman? One of my grandmothers? I don't know. She sang and cut.

I listened to the scissors click through my fingernails.

This woke me up for good.

■ ■ ■

Pursuit. Human beings are accustomed to pursuit. We pursue, or we are pursued. This is exciting to us. Most of us enjoy being frightened, scared a little bit, up until the fear turns to real panic.

My dreams pursue me in waking. I wish they didn't. The thing I am most afraid of, Q, is that I will finally be caught in a dream that won't ever end. When I am endlessly pursued, constant prey. Insanity.

■ ■ ■

When I was little, crying in the middle of the night because of my dreams, my dad would come in, and I swear he'd be shining. It was probably just the hall light behind him, but he was lit up. He'd put his hand on my cheek and shush me back to sleep. Sometimes he'd hum, and his deep voice would put me right out. If I was totally terrified or sobbing, he'd lie down next to me, and rest his hand on my chest, and I could smell his smell. Man smell. You know what I mean? Soap, the day, his beard. His lips would be right up close to my ear. He'd count backward from a hundred in a whisper, and I'd fall back into a boring sleep before he made it down to ninety—.

And here we are, heaven, otherwise known as Geno's.

■ ■ ■

We can eat and walk, can't we? Sure. You can do it. If I sit now, I may not want to stand back up. Remember? No sleep.

I want to take you with me, Q, all over. I want you to get tired. I want you to feel strong and tired, and I want you to see things you haven't seen before. I want you to feel pleasure.

Like the pleasure of Geno's. Baked goods and meat. Salami. Oh, salami—.

I don't know why I order by the third of a pound.

Want some more? Eat, eat.

■ ■ ■

I want to thank you for letting me order your pistachio cannoli and macchiato for you. A big guy like you letting little me talk for you. Thank you. I know I'll need to hear your voice before we're home. Until then—.

Moaning is definitely acceptable. See? Incredible.

You already know more than you did half an hour ago.

■ ■ ■

I wasn't very far from home, a mile and change, but I had never been to Geno's. Already, my world had expanded; I did know more, and this embarrassed me a bit. I felt less like I was seventeen than seven, with my big sister showing me a world totally new to me. Sometimes, though, this is the feeling we have when talking to someone whose brain and imagination are a little wilder than ours. We have the feeling there's a whole lot we haven't learned or thought or seen. We feel we haven't explored the world. We feel a bit behind. It's hard to remember the person who's wilder might actually be the person who's in trouble.

I was happy to eat a little, since I didn't know when I would eat again. My fate was tied to Nest's, my comfort to her comfort.

The cannoli was incredible. Go to Geno's.

■ ■ ■

I brought a couple books, Q. That's why you're carrying the backpack. That, and to hold whatever we find. You're a beast of burden. Not that you have a ring through your nose—.

I never pick up anything I can't carry a long way. No. That's not true. I once carried home a café chair left on the curb. I just sat down whenever I needed to rest. Ridiculous. It's in my room. And I carried a mirror—a crazy wood frame, all carved, with gold leaf—I carried that a long time before I got tired and hid it. Every day, every other day, I'd lug it, hide it, lug it, hide it. I did this, I don't know, ten days, two weeks, but I never got it home. The last day: gone. Someone found my hiding place. Took my mirror. I dragged that thing around and.

I brought home a nest once, a real nest. It had feathers and pieces of newspaper and tinfoil, or maybe it was a gum wrapper, and all the woven twigs. I brought it home because it had a fortune from a fortune cookie stitched, I guess, into the bottom. *You are endowed with strength of purpose and energy of will.* It must have kept that bird going for days. So motivational. So inspiring.

Sometimes, I don't even want to carry a water bottle. A little aluminum bottle can feel like an anchor. Or like the whole ship.

The books.

Wait. Want my last half muffin?

No, I'll give it to that man. I wish I had more. My father taught me to carry food to give away. But today I was thinking about you, and I forgot—.

Half a muffin.

■ ■ ■

Did you hear him, Q, when he took the muffin? You kind of drifted off, backed away. Maybe you were too far to hear.

Only half a muffin, but—.

He said, "'For now I ask no more than the justice of eating.'"

He pushed the muffin into his mouth.

"Wait," I said. "Did you just come up with that?"

He shook his head: "Pafflo Neroofa."

"Pablo Neruda?"

He nodded and I waited for him to swallow. "Neruda, yeah." Then: "Have a good day, Supergirl."

I like running into people who like poetry almost as

much as I like running into poets. You never know when it'll happen.

■ ■ ■

Who do you think is more ashamed, Q, the guy living in his parents' basement or the guy living on the curb? Who knows how much shame anybody feels inside? But who does the world think should be more ashamed? The guy who doesn't do anything with himself, doesn't work or— but lives off his parents and doesn't have to worry about how to survive, doesn't worry about success or failure? Is that man more of a loser, more shameful than the homeless man or beggar who really has no one and may be sick or very unlucky, maybe starving to death?

I don't know. The thing is, we don't even think about the guy in the basement, unless we personally know the guy in the basement. But when we see a homeless man on the street, a stranger kicked in the teeth by life, we probably don't know him, but we think about him. Automatically. We think about him, at least for a second, and we feel something for him. We feel sorry for him, or we get angry, or we laugh, or run away. The guy in the street, like that guy with half my muffin, shames me, shames us, shames society more than the guy in the basement. Maybe that's why you backed off: shame.

The homeless man's out in the open. He's our nightmare, our mistake, and he's a lot like us, but not. Who makes us feel worse, the guy in the basement or the guy in the gutter?

■ ■ ■

I can't seem to get to the books. I keep starting. But hunger and quotes and stories and starving men and salami. Have I told you what my favorite food is—?

I nearly went off the tracks again.

Books. Books, books, books.

I found *The Origin of Species*—Darwin, you know?—in the basement. My mother's name so neat at the top right of the title page over the year: *Martha Lind 1983*, when she was seventeen. Seventeen, so I thought I'd.

Yeah.

Do you put your name in books?

Isaac Kew. I. Kew. Or the letters, *I. K.*? That would look strong; I can see it, strong and tall, like you.

Strong and tall, and not too smart for your own good. No, I mean, you have half a chance to live life without too much sadness and crippling self-doubt. People with excess intelligence, high IQs over 120, 125? Screwed. The higher you go, the worse off you are. These people often fail at life and end up—ha!—living in the basement. Or walking the streets at all hours, talking nonstop, unable to sleep—.

Oops.

Whatever.

You're bedrock, Q.

■ ■ ■

Maybe my mother had a reason. To write her name in books. But what could that reason be? My mom's the youngest of six, four girls, two boys. I think she received so many hand-me-downs that when she got something for herself, for her and no one else, not read, worn, or discarded by someone before her, it mattered. It had real value. A key chain, a handbag, a book, a boyfriend. A teacher gave the *Origin* to Martha, a prize for being the best student in eighth-grade science. She was thirteen, but she didn't put her name in the book for four years. Coincidentally, my mom gave up science and even college when she met my father. And when did she meet him? When she was seventeen.

So maybe Martha Lind, who fell in love with Vladimir Fitzgerald, a graduate student in physics and fully seven years older—they met, Martha and Fitz and. Mm-hmm. Fitz had to wait for my mother to turn eighteen before they could get married. My grandmother's rules, apparently, my mother's mother. Violet, or Dye as my mother calls her, told her youngest baby, "You've got to graduate high school. He can wait for that, can't he?"

Maybe Martha gathered up the few things she called her own and wrote her name as she'd always known it before she went off with the love of her life and never looked back. Martha wasn't beautiful, but she had that high forehead, filled with brains, and her voice, and her teeth. Have you seen my mother's teeth? Her smile? You could find your way through the darkest hell. Fitz might have been considered out of her league in the looks department, sort of like you're out of mine.

Do you think we should let ourselves fall in love with someone from a different—stratum? Dangerous. I don't need to tell you why. If you're from Earth but you love someone from the moon, you might try to make it work, but one of you might always be short of breath or a little light-headed, a wee bit homesick.

I'm babbling again.

Martha wanted very much to marry Fitz and take his name. But she'd barely ever owned anything, including her own name, she was so young. She packed up her room—it was her room finally after her sister, my aunt Lu, left for college a couple years earlier; Martha packed and put everything to one side. She wanted to move as soon as possible into her grown-up life, no joke. She wanted privacy with Fitz. She wanted her own home.

You can see her right now, packing up her belongings, maybe a bit early, since she wouldn't turn eighteen for three months and, as it happened, Fitz the Physicist wouldn't propose for two more years. He was midway through the dissertation that would settle his life when he had a crisis of confidence. He thought, *I'm not going to get through this thing; I hate physics,* and decided that would be a good time to ask Martha to marry him: who knows why? Martha was a month shy of twenty when they eloped.

But I'm thinking of my mother at seventeen, in love and restless.

Martha wrote her name in Darwin—neat, so neat—and the date underneath. Then she put him in a box and waited.

■ ■ ■

I've made myself hot and sad thinking about Martha and her books.

My mother—.

The time has come for me to take off the flannel. Excited? I know you. Every part of me is in motion when I walk. That's what you say. It makes me sound like I have no control over my limbs. Like with every step, my foot touches off a land mine. I think you mean I wiggle. My dad used to tell me I didn't so much walk as sashay.

You like it.

■ ■ ■

I'm not entirely sure why my mother read the *Origin*. She told me she read it all the time, took it around with her. Tons of marginalia back to front, her little notes and doodles and underlinings and. You've got it on your back right now.

I brought two, though, two books. Darwin and one other for your pleasure. Here were the choices.

Wind, Sand and Stars, which you know about already.

Summerhill: A Radical Approach to Child Rearing, by A. S. Neill, foreword by Erich Fromm. I found it on Darwin's left. Another of my mom's: same inscription, same date, lots of notes, but I don't know how she got it or why. Everything was about child rearing back in the day. Dr. Spock, heard of him? My parents have him on the shelf, too, on Darwin's right. *Summerhill*'s a trip, though. It's all about the balance in the child-parent relationship. "Freedom without license." That's a quote. There's a whole section about sex, which, curiously, my mother left unmarked. None of her usual notes, drawings, exclamation points. Silence. Maybe she found it in her parents' basement. It's old: 1960.

Remember that line about rabbits and dogs? Seems like ages ago. Where there are rabbits, there shall be dogs. That's from *Flush*. It's a biography from the dog's point of view. Seriously. And not just any dog. Oh no. Elizabeth Barrett Browning's. Do you know her? Poet? "How do I love thee? Let me count the ways." She wrote that, but she didn't write *Flush*. Virginia Woolf did, and then she drowned herself. Not immediately after. As if she got to the end of that funky book about Flush and said, "What have I done?" and decided life wasn't worth living. I mean, sometime later, she committed suicide.

Flush the dog talks about all sorts of things: city life, love, mind. Stream of consciousness, a brain uninterrupted, sort of like what you get to enjoy right now, on this walk, but an animal's, a cocker spaniel's. Crazy smart book and crazy weird.

Those were the choices. Adventure, education and child rearing, or weirdness? Or something altogether different?

I can hear you quietly asking yourself in a tiny voice inside your head, a tiny, tinkling voice, totally surprising for someone so big: What did she bring? What did she bring?

MILE THREE

The voice inside my head sounds nothing like a wee fairy. It doesn't tinkle.

Or?

Maybe by the time my thoughts made it through bone, skin, and air, all the way to Nest's ear, they chimed like a fairy. I have no doubt Nest could hear me thinking. She gave the impression of being more than a little superhuman. And by superhuman, I mean mad. Mad as in lunatic.

Lunatic or not, I didn't care.

What did she bring? What did she bring?

That moment, that morning, full sun and warming up, I listened to Nest's every word.

What did she bring?

I'd have to wait to find out. First things first: a labyrinth.

■ ■ ■

My father isn't always human. He has his Angers. And his Angers make him terrible. He rages and storms. He mutters under his breath. He curses and judges and grinds his teeth and. On his best days, my dad terrifies you, his voice and scowl. You haven't seen him as the Minotaur.

I don't find it easy to talk about this. I've watched my father froth at the mouth and gouge his own eyes.

My father, the Minotaur. Man with a bull's head: horns and giant nostrils. What breed of head? If I had to pick, I'd go with Scottish Highland. I looked it up in a book of breeds once, what my father looks like. Wide, curving horns; mop of ginger bangs; ginger beard; trapezoidal white nose: very handsome cattle. But he's a Minotaur, a monster, walking back and forth, around and around, at the center of his labyrinth, waiting to kill.

I don't know what starts the Angers. My mother won't

say, if she even knows herself. She tells me my father's a haunted man.

"Haunted?" I say. "By what?"

She shrugs.

"You love him," I say. "You've known him for so long. You married him. How can you not know?"

My mother furrows a little. Still puzzling it out, right?

"It's some kind of torture," she says, "but I don't know for what. He frightens me. What he feels, Nest, the strength of it, frightens me. His agony."

"He scares me, too, sometimes."

"I know he does," she says and kisses my forehead. "He's a passionate man."

"It's like you always tell me. No one kinder than Dad, and no one rougher."

■ ■ ■

Watch it, Q. Didn't you see that car? Pay attention. Don't get killed while we're walking. What sense would that make? Listen and think, but watch, too. In this city, traffic lights and stop signs are only suggestions.

This city. It's pretty much frustrated chaos. Like a Minotaur.

The Minotaur rarely shows up during the day. But the transformations: I would watch my father transform in full light. The Angers come over him. His eyes turn black. He shudders and snorts and sighs. His horns break out of his head, and his skull grows new bone. His big, long, heavy bull jaw. He grinds his teeth.

My poor dad. He'd work so hard all day to keep himself under control in front of me. He'd try not to scare us, my mom and me. And Julius? One hundred and eighteen pounds of Rottweiler—my beautiful, gentle puppy—hides under the dining table when my father starts grunting and mumbling.

My father drops his head and waves it back and forth, shaking invisible flies, and he heaves. Exhausted or overcome. The sighing. The transformation must be so painful. Getting less and less human over hours. His blood all thick and hot. His headaches—from the horns breaking his head. Imagine if you grew horns, and your mind turned into a furnace, and your heart compressed into a diamond the size of a fingernail.

His voice deepens even more, but he barely speaks. He looks at me from under his bull's eyebrows, no smile.

Death. I'm his enemy. My mother's his enemy. My father, monster, has no friend left in the world. No love.

■ ■ ■

Late at night, when my father's fully Minotaur, he'll leave the house for hours.

"He walks," my mother says. I'm lying in bed next to her. I'm six, seven, eight, nine, ten, eleven, and on those nights my father hasn't said good night or anything at all to me. He looked at me like.

All murder and anger.

Then he left, gone. So I got into bed with my mother.

"Doesn't he get scared?" I say. I'm little, you know? I say something like: "It's dark. Mean people are out at night."

"Your dad can take care of himself just fine," my mother tells me. "He's—intimidating. But he—. When he's away from us, he doesn't have anything holding him back."

"Will he hurt us?"

"Never," my mother says, but she holds me anyway, against the fear.

■ ■ ■

Night. Not too many people on the street. The city's a labyrinth. The Minotaur hides his head and horns in the shadows. He punches brick and concrete. He punches trees. He sharpens his horns against granite.

He knocks over trash cans, kicks them down alleys—thunder and cymbals; he bellows now and then. No one dares go to the window. Something awful is tearing up the skinny space between buildings. Better to let it go, stay in bed. The riot has to end soon.

■ ■ ■

At some point toward morning, the Minotaur dies. Or falls asleep. The Angers disappear, and my dad gets back to himself. When he's human again, he limps out of the labyrinth into the real world and home. Hunched over and. Like he's been beaten up all night, from the inside. He's in real pain, wincing, checking the bones in his face, his cheeks and eyebrows. He's touching his head all over, delicately. Every inch is a bruise. Tiny fractures. From the transformation. He sits at the dining room table, exhausted, embarrassed, ashamed, and so sad. But he's a man again. Quiet, quiet, quiet.

The Angers defeat him. They make him into a broken boy.

I'll hear him pull out a chair, and I'll go to him. He's a mess. I'll pour him something to drink. I'll give him a hug, and that's when I notice his hands. Huge and swollen and cut and bruised, torn up and bloody from all the punching. I want to tell him he'll break his hand someday. I love my father. I want to tell him I love him. But I'm afraid even the smallest word will cut the skin around his eyes or ears and make him bleed.

What does this have to do with me?

My father, I think I told you, used to take me on walks at night. Not on his Minotaur walks. Not ever. Gentle walks, the two of us. I was pretty young when we started walking together: seven. I remember. I had a terrible night, the first real terrible night when I couldn't sleep.

My father heard me crying. I think he's awake to me, always, even now. I've tried to catch him asleep ten thousand times. In the mornings, I'd tiptoe into my parents' room, and my dad would raise his hand and wave. My mother? A log. Occasionally, I find my father on the couch or in a chair with his eyes shut, but I never get close enough to catch him asleep. Something in him hears or smells me, and he says, "What can I do for you, Nest?" He doesn't even open his eyes.

Seven years old, almost eight. That first horrible night,

the bloody dreams: my father came in to help me back to sleep, except I. I couldn't sleep. I wouldn't. Nothing he tried helped. After an hour, he said, "O the cunning wiles that creep / In thy little heart asleep! / When thy little heart doth wake, / Then the dreadful light shall break."

"What?" I had no idea what he was talking about.

"Pardon me?" he said, correcting me. I've never been too polite. "William Blake. Get dressed, something warm. We're taking a walk."

"Isn't it late?"

"Someone once said, 'Only thoughts won by walking are valuable.' Now come on."

So we walked in the middle of the night.

■ ■ ■

We didn't go very far that first time. He took me to the diner—Stern's, your favorite—since it's twenty-four-hour. What's it, a half mile from my house? He bought me pancakes. It's around midnight. Midnight's the actual middle of the night to a kid. Pancakes and sausage and a vanilla milk shake. He said, "Want my help with that, honey?" Pretty much, he ate it, but he got it for me.

We talked. He told me the history of the diner. It

wasn't always twenty-four-hour. It changed in the late, I don't know, a long time ago, when people called it the Mayor's. The mayor at the time had grown up in the neighborhood, and he'd come to the diner once a week around two in the morning for a sandwich. Always liverwurst on rye with mustard and onions, a sour pickle, and a chocolate soda. His chauffeur sat with him, and he'd order, too. "Same, no onions, no mustard, no pickle, hold the liverwurst, wheat, toasted." A comedian. Oh, and the chauffeur didn't want a soda. He ordered a regular coffee, which meant with milk and sugar. Stern himself would make the plates and serve them.

The mayor talked to whoever walked in that time of night. Friends, enemies, night owls, the lonely. He treated some lucky person to a coffee or a plate of eggs, Salisbury steak, pastrami, whatever they wanted. He called the whole spectacle Night Court. Or maybe not that, but something like that. The mayor sat there for an hour, hour and a half. Then he left without paying. The chauffeur paid. "One day," the driver would say, "I'll get that son of a gun to pull out his own wallet."

"You'll have to wait until I'm voted out," the mayor would say, waiting by the door. "My money's the taxpayer's."

"So's mine," the chauffeur grumbled.

A year or so later, the mayor died in office. For a long time, some folks like me, not too well off in the head, swore they saw the ghost head right on through the glass door for his liverwurst. People still called Stern's the Mayor's, even after he died. They'd show up, 2:00 A.M. Not just one night, but night after night. Every night. Patrons, right? Diners. Drunks. Dollar bills with mouths. They'd pound on the door, yelling up to the Sterns, who lived overhead.

"Let us in, let us in," shouted the hungry masses. "What's good for the mayor's good for us."

Unless the liverwurst and onion killed him. You couldn't pay me enough.

"Let us in, let us in."

"Okay, stop banging," Old Stern shouted down from the second-floor window. "Hold your horses." Then, he turned to his son and said, "What are you waiting for, Junior? Get down there already."

The people ate their fill.

"There it is," my father said. "Stern's: twenty-four hours, seven days a week."

He took over the milk shake and stirred it with a straw.

"Once," he went on, "right here, in this booth, I nearly asked your mother to marry me. Luckily, Nest, I came to my senses." He sucked the last of the shake. Loud, with the straw.

"What?" I said.

"Pardon? I'm saying, my little girl, whatever you do, don't ever let a man propose to you in a restaurant."

I'm seven.

"An eatery of any kind. Don't let it happen."

"Okay, Daddy."

"Promise me."

"I promise."

He handed out some wisdom about bad proposals, the dull and impulsive, and good proposals, the true surprises, the grand gestures; I can't remember exactly what. Then he leaned in close. "Remember," he said, low and serious, "even the best meals end in the bathroom next morning."

Yup. That's what he said. I thought this was hilarious. The word *bathroom* killed me. I'm in second grade, so—.

He asked for the bill, and we walked home, holding hands.

■ ■ ■

Home, and my mother dead asleep.

"Pajamas and bed, Nest."

Ever respectful, my father waited outside my room until I called him in. He pulled my covers up and kissed my cheek.

"That was fun, wasn't it?" he said.

"I want to go again," I said.

"Next time you can't sleep, we'll walk."

My father and I, we walked a lot.

■ ■ ■

Angers, Minotaur, walks, Stern's and the mayor, terror, milk shakes, proposals, and.

We're going into the park. The cars will disappear. You won't notice it right away, the silence. It sneaks up on you. And just when you're about to say, "You hear that? No cars," the birds will come and the wind. You'll hear the leaves crash into the ground, our footsteps, and the sun pouring down the trees. All that peacenoise.

Chickadees and nuthatches. *Vroom, vroom* to *tweet, tweet.*

I'm taking you somewhere important, Q. Important to me. Past the carousel and the old stables, almost out the other side of the park. My walking grounds, my labyrinth.

My labyrinth.

A Chimaera, though. Chimaeras don't haunt labyrinths. I'm just making the connection. Like the Minotaur, I would need a place to prowl.

■ ■ ■

I stopped sleeping in bed with my mother when the Minotaur stopped frightening me. The Minotaur stopped frightening me when I—.

Thirteen when my Angers came. My Angers and my period. Blood and rage and.

My Chimaera.

My father has his nostrils and horns. I'm three-faced: lion, goat, and snake. Saber tooth, split hoof, and cobra hood. Roaring and bleating, running, breathing fire. Her six stone eyes, solid turquoise.

Body of a lion. A goat's neck and head and one leg growing out of my back. A snake for a tail. A furnace in my heart.

Sometimes my Chimaera is silent. Silent as the grave. Or almost silent. Crouched and tense, coiled, panting a little.

Pretty picture, right?

They're not connected. My period and my Angers—.
Sometimes, but.

I started bleeding, and. Oh my God, so painful. They're easier now, like you need to know. I'm saying I don't automatically get the Angers when I bleed. That's important. One doctor, a man—figures—tried to tell me I suffer from exceptionally serious PMS. So insulting. I was fourteen, and he wanted to put me on the pill, to try—.

I can't talk about it.

My father transforms into the Minotaur over hours. He suffers. My Chimaera arrives between breaths. So quick, the fell swoop. Lion, goat, and snake. Hardly painful at all.

She's a fraction and a sum. A fragment of everything I am, and the sum of all the tiny dark gods inside of me speaking at the same time, shouting over each other. Totally maddening: the infinite rudeness of the gods.

My father said he'd walk miles and miles at night with his Angers. He would end up in places with no memory of how he'd arrived. By the end, he'd be calm again—at least for a little while.

I walk when I walk, but I wait until sunrise. I'm not like my father, walking in shadows. I've always wanted light.

My father's walked with my Chimaera. Right next to me—her—without a word. It didn't start out that way. I mean, we'd be walking, just fine, and something would come over me. She'd slither and climb right up out of me. No warning. We'd walk and walk until the Angers left me, and I'd start to cry. Then I'd shake. I could barely stand, and I'd lean on my dad. He'd hold me up or carry me the rest of the way home.

"Why did you give this to me?" I asked him once. I was holding on to his arm, so tired but still thinking. Sad, like—. "I mean the Angers."

"I never thought," he said. "My mother gave them to me, but."

I cried and cried. "You shouldn't have had a child if there was even the tiniest chance."

What could he say?

"Look at me. I'm a Chimaera—."

Nothing.

■ ■ ■

I walk through the front door, all girl again, and collapse on the couch. My Chimaera is back inside, sleeping in my chest, behind my heart. I've stopped crying finally. My father evaporates; my mother appears. She brings me tea and covers me up with a blanket.

"This takes a lot out of you." My mother's smoothing my hair. "The mood, the inner strife. We couldn't know this would happen."

"It doesn't make it any easier," I say. We've had this conversation over five years already.

"You were born from the best of us, Nest. Not from the worst. I can't claim to understand what either you or your father endures. It's a suffering for all of us. You most of all."

"A suffering."

"Is there anything else to call it?"

■ ■ ■

My father doesn't turn into the Minotaur every day of every month. He's not a Jekyll and Hyde. Have you read that, by the way? *The Strange Case of Dr. Jekyll and Mr. Hyde*? Holy crap, it's scary, isn't it? But it's even more depressing than frightening.

My dad's not on a schedule, like a werewolf at full moon. The Minotaur's not a constant, not a machine. It's hard to say. If you average it out, maybe twice a month, but. My father will go for weeks without the Angers. In March and April, though, he might hit the streets as the

Minotaur three times in a week. And October? Look out. Tomorrow morning, I might be boiling an egg for my father five minutes after he's come home from the labyrinth; ordering him to drink a glass of juice; rubbing his temples, right where his horns dissolved. He won't talk. And you can't come over. He won't let you see him like that, with his eyes still black and sad.

■ ■ ■

As for me. My Angers, my Chimaera, they're always faster than the Minotaur, always more complicated, especially now. Angers are only a part of what I—.

There's the anger and the joy and the sadness and the inspiration and the tiredness and the energy, all the energy, enough energy to row a boat from here to Istanbul, to walk around the earth twice, to love you long after I'm dead.

■ ■ ■

Can you love my Chimaera? Can you love melted iron and a comet? She's the Equator and the South Pole. She's a desert and the bottom of the ocean. Completely wild.

A bit deadly. Horn, fangs, snow, salt, and sand. Totally strange and mysterious. She can't speak.

No, she can speak; she doesn't like it much, though. She prefers screeching.

I don't actually know what she talks about, what she says. My parents tell me she asks after my health. I think that's a euphemism.

My Chimaera may show up any moment, even midsentence. You might see her before the end of our walk. If you do, remain calm. Do not engage. If she asks you a question, do not answer. Do not run. You're a tall drink of water, so let her drink. If she wants, let her take you here, where we walk, the two of us, just a girl and her Chimaera, among the graves.

■ ■ ■

The dead cemetery I'd heard about, but had never seen. At the edge of the park, neglected and miserable, talking to itself. Sort of like the madman in the attic, almost entirely forgotten.

"There's a gate," Nest said. "What's not to like about an abandoned cemetery?"

The gate was choked with vines, and we had to slide

through sideways. Ancient stones and mounds and markers. Trees.

We stood on opposite sides of an ancient sunlit grave, facing each other. Was anybody else even there? No. We were alone, Nest and I. No sign of her Chimaera.

The Chimaera. Lion, goat, serpent—. I would have to see the beast myself to understand. But the only way to the Chimaera was through Nest's Angers. Her Angers twisted— no, even now, they twist her up. They transform her into something terrible, and she suffers. The Chimaera arrives when Nest suffers. What happens to the girl?

I stole glances at Nest; she stared off at the trees. I heard the birch and cypress sighing behind me.

"I was watching a yellow leaf shaking on the end of a branch. Behind you: see? Even if that leaf survives winter, it will give itself up to a bud in spring."

Nest.

I wanted to say her name.

"I think that fact alone, that the leaf might get through winter to die in spring, that fact alone separates earth from heaven."

Even if I could've answered, even if I had pretended to make sense of what she was talking about, I wouldn't have said anything more than her name.

Nest.

On one of my walks with my father, he told me why he and my mother had to be together, even why she stayed with him and with the Minotaur.

"The Japanese," he said, "actually have a phrase for what your mom and I experienced when we met. *Koi no yokan*. The sense on first meeting that two people will fall in love. Both know a future love is inevitable."

Didn't this exact same thing happen between us, Q? We've never talked about it. I felt it, even when I was telling you my name began with a silent *P*, but I pretended it never happened. How could anyone—? It's hopeless, right? I'm crazy, I have a Chimaera inside me, but. It's inevitable, the love. That's the point.

And here we are, in this cemetery. My Chimaera is a secret Chimaera most of the time, until.

Nest.

I can hear you. You want to talk. You want to say something kind to me. You've always loved me, I know it. You're kind and patient, and you've waited until this exact day. I've waited, too.

Don't speak, Q. Keep going with me. Walk with me over the graves.

We drifted among the headstones, reading one after another. Powell, Dyer, Guthrie, Drown, and so on, until we came across a marker sticking up at an angle from between the roots of a tree.

"I think this is the oldest stone," Nest said. "I'm almost sure of it, except for the Quaker markers that have no words at all. And you can't be sure who might have been buried here before there was a cemetery. It's a nice spot. I imagine people have buried their own here for thousands of years. A hundred wars might have been fought on this pretty little hill, people killed and killed and killed, and we'll never know. But this stone belongs to a man whose name we can read. An early American, right? Maybe a veteran of the Revolution. Or a Loyalist. He might have cried for the king every day of his life. Who knows?"

Nest crouched down next to the stone and traced the letters with her fingers. "Obadiah Pilk," she said. "Died 1798." For a minute, she fingered a long, mossy crack that ran diagonal. "Some people die hard, Q."

The color of the sky was the color of a wasp's wing. Rain after all.

On our slow way out of the cemetery, Nest stopped me.

I know how he died. Pilk, I mean. That crack in the stone. I could tell right through my fingers. He was cutting trees, and one fell on him. He suffered a long time before he died. The whole weight of a tree broke him. Every rib. His hip. His back. A skinny branch went through his eye. But he died slowly, with a leaf tickling his ear, torturing him the whole time. With his good eye, he watched a little bit of sky through the leaves. The light fading and fading, the way it is now, until the light, as Mr. Pilk understood it, left.

We stood there under the black-brown sky, the wind picking up, and the more I looked at Nest, the more I believed her. Chimaera, Pilk, Minotaur, all of it.

Koi no yokan.

I admit I didn't really know what Nest was trying to tell me, except she was afraid of her mind, and afraid of herself. Afraid of her Chimaera and Angers and going totally insane. Afraid of dying insane. Afraid of going unloved and feared. But she still had hope.

You believe me, Q. I know you do.

Give praise to the magic of a cemetery.

MILE FOUR

We're inevitable, Q. Funny thing is, you don't even know my first name, the name I keep secret. But you're learning my secrets, aren't you.

Yes, and—.

I might want to hear you say my full name.

■ ■ ■

I listen to my mother when she talks in her sleep. I call it talking Between, capital B. It's a real place for her, Between, even though it's only a horizon: sky above, earth below; not here, not there; not awake, not asleep. She'll come out with something random, ask a question or. About this and that, whatever's on her mind. Most of the time, it's funny. Funny or not, though, it's honest. Nobody can edit what's said Between.

It goes like this.

"Mom?" Maybe she's on the couch. Maybe the Minotaur left her behind, and she drifted off while watching TV. "Mom, time for bed."

And she says, "Did you butter the toast?"

Or "I don't have anything to trade for a diamond."

Or "Did you take Jefferson out?" Jefferson was the huge Alsatian-Lab-mastodon hybrid my mother grew up with. A gentle giant, like you and my dad. He died when I was two, after he taught me how to walk. I'd hold on to his ears, his tail, his tusks, and—.

My mother will occasionally tell stories with her eyes closed.

"That skinny cowboy danced with me the whole night. A real cowboy, boots, hat, bolo tie, the whole package. Mustache. He even called me little lady. I was fourteen. Where did he come from? He was as handsome as his horse, and he wore leather gloves and carried a rope."

It's kind of spooky and funny at the same time.

Occasionally, we go back and forth. Like last week, she said, "Nest, sweetie, help me load that app on my phone."

"What app?" I said.

"The scale. So I can weigh myself."

I started laughing.

"I'm serious," she said. "I can stand on my phone and—"

She overheard herself, some hidden part of her with ears, and she laughed. "I'm so ridiculous."

The weirdest thing is she had no memory of anything the next morning, none of it, not even laughing with me.

■ ■ ■

I hear very little of what my mom says Between. That pleasure goes to my father, and he tells me only what makes him laugh, the sweet things, or the childlike, never what upsets him: my mother's confessions, her fears or disappointments or sadness.

I sometimes hear the sadness.

"I'm very sad," she'll say.

"Why are you very sad?" I'll say.

"I don't know."

"You don't know? Are you sad about me or Dad?"

"Yes. But I have to sleep."

Nothing more.

Sometimes, she'll cry Between, and I'll be the one to wake her and hold her until the sadness falls asleep with her.

My mother and her Between.

"You'll always love me, won't you, Nest?"

"Yes, Mom."

"Just say yes."

"Yes."

"And your father, too?"

Or "Julius always smells pretty after a bath."

"He hates it," I say. "He gets embarrassed."

"He's neutered, right?"

"Yup."

"Dumb dog."

Or "Dad will get home safe. Nothing can hurt him. He's so handsome and crazy and—."

Long pause.

"And?" Me again. "Mom? He's so handsome and crazy and?"

She says something I don't catch, and I'm scared the thread's cut. "Mom? Dad's so handsome and—?"

"And he's a physicist."

The next day, I have to remind her. "Mom, last night you said—," and she rolls her eyes.

"It's embarrassing." She shakes her head. "What was it this time?"

She never remembers.

"Today, a man in the grocery store asked me why I let your father talk to me so harshly."

I'm uncomfortable, a little afraid.

"I don't know what he heard. I was surrounded by misted vegetables and ten thousand apples. Your father had walked off without me, upset. Trembling and haunted."

"He does that," I said. "He's trying to protect you from the Angers."

"He was a good-looking man, younger than me. He had a cabbage in his hand, or a couple of yams. And I thought, Maybe a guy like this wouldn't talk to me the way my husband sometimes does. He'd never scare me or make me worry all night."

I couldn't know where this would go. What would my mother confess Between?

"But your father was suffering. He didn't mean to hurt me, and he was only gruff, not insulting. I smiled politely at the man and turned to the bananas or the tomatoes or whatever."

"Did Dad catch any of—?"

"No. That would've been it for the buttinsky."

"Buttinsky?"

"With his dimples and his bok choy. If he thought I was in danger from your father, wouldn't he have defended me? If he were brave? But he waited until I was alone before planting his seed. Trying to steal a little ground, right? Dad's alpha. And this guy, with his coward's heart, this beta, didn't know anything about my Vladimir, his trouble, his love for me, or my love for him, or about you, or all our love."

And that was it. The end.

Sleep came down.

■ ■ ■

It doesn't sound like this exactly, my mother's Between talk. She's mushy, and her tongue's not really into it. Her gentle voice is softer than—I don't know—. Her voice is baby's breath. You have to imagine her sleepslur, the pauses, my having to ask her a hundred times to repeat herself, hoping she won't go to sleep or fully wake in the middle. But all that doesn't translate to good storytelling. I have to stitch it together a bit. And I have to—elaborate.

■ ■ ■

I know, my first name. We're getting there.

So. The day's done, everything's behind her, and my mother closes her eyes. She's still and quiet. Then, Between, she gets chatty.

I have a theory about it. It started when she was a girl. Being the youngest and on the quiet side, Martha didn't talk much and was heard even less. My aunts and uncles, they're all loud and. No one ever really listened for the runt. At night, after the crowded family shut up—finally, thank God—Martha talked maybe a whole day's worth as she fell asleep. To no one in particular, only herself.

That's my theory.

Everybody needs to talk and be heard. Even if you're the only one listening.

■ ■ ■

My mother gave me the name Nest. My parents have told me this a thousand times. It came to her a week before I was born. She was in a motel bed with my father, Between, and:

"We have to name her Nest."

She was talking straight into my father's chest, and he didn't think he'd heard right.

"What was that?" he said and lifted her head a little. A very bright and shocking moon slashed through the curtains, marking the bed and floor and my mother's cheek.

"We have to name her Nest."

"You know we're having a girl?"

"I want her to have the name of a princess-mother."

"Nest?" my father said.

"Nest." Then my pregnant mother went to sleep. And the next morning, for once, she remembered.

■ ■ ■

There was a Princess Nest, only one in the history of the world, not counting fairies. In Wales, right after the Norman Conquest. The name Fitzgerald—son of Gerald— follows a line all the way back to Nest and her husband. All the British royal Tudors and Stuarts, all the poor and rich Irish with that name, John Fitzgerald Kennedy, and my father, Vladimir Fitzgerald, come down from Nest, all of them cousins—.

You have no idea what I'm saying.

The human genome, Q. I'm your cousin, in a way, and we're both cousins to Einstein, Nat Turner, Cleopatra, Susan B. Anthony, Ashoka, Tecumseh, Moses, Amelia Earhart, Shakespeare, the Dalai Lama, Old Stern, his rabbi, and his rabbi's wife and son, if the rabbi even had a wife and son—how should I know? We're related by chromosome to Athena, the Sun King, Shaka, Quetzalcoatl, Saint Dymphna, Saladin, Genghis Khan, the lady who just walked by, and.

Nest.

Everyone thinks my parents were high or hippies. I don't think my mother's ever been high in her life, but she is a history buff. High on history, like me.

You keeping up, honey?

■ ■ ■

God, the air's heavy. Do you feel it? There's a cloud like a bag of hammers on my back. It'll rain, for sure, but we're close to the university—.

And here it comes. Huge drops, almost like water balloons.

How fast can you walk a half mile?

■ ■ ■

Nest is my middle name.

"We can call her Nest," my dad told my mom in the hospital. "At home, if you like. But she might want a more common first name. For official purposes. Or in school."

Until he grew ten feet tall, until the Angers and Minotaur, my father had been bullied for his name and for everything else. He'd been named for Lenin by two deeply committed American Communists, and, well, he grew up during the Cold War. He worried for me. He didn't want me to suffer. And my mother, still kind of drunk after giving birth, agreed.

She regrets it Between. "I never should have let that happen," she's said with her eyes closed, all her dreams sneaking up. "You're Nest."

"Yup. I'm Nest."

"Princess-mother Nest."

I'm sure she says the same thing to my father: "She's Nest, the mother of generations." My father, I'm sure, clenches his teeth and feels ashamed again and again. He'll never live it down.

But they named me after a powerful and beautiful queen, a second mother of generations.

I'm Eleanor.

Pleased to meet you.

■ ■ ■

Eleanor of Aquitaine was born forty years after Nest. Queen to Louis VII of France and Henry II of England. She was beautiful and survived everything the twelfth century could throw at a woman: disease, childbirth, war, prison, betrayal, and widowhood. A kiss if you can tell me the names of Eleanor's two most famous sons, both kings of England.

—?—

Think Robin Hood.

—??—

Lionheart—? The Magna Carta—?

—???—

No kiss for you.

■ ■ ■

Oh, Q. I know what will keep your mind off the rain and rush.

Wait for it—.

Trivia. You know, like *Jeopardy!* You're not allowed to talk. Answer, if you can, with your eyes.

— . . . —

Let's start with this. Easy. The category is Music.

Who's missing from this list of the original members of One Direction: Niall Horan, Zayn Malik, Liam Payne, Louis Tomlinson, and?

—?—

Hint: I hate them all together.

—!—

I can see the gleam in your eye. It's right there, tip of the tongue, but—.

—?!—

Nope. Not quite. You know, but you don't know.

I think that sums up the fun and unfun of trivia: the knowing and not knowing. It feels good when you have the answer. Sometimes, though, you really don't know or you're totally off the mark, and sometimes, you know— you really, really know—but you just can't quite get there. You can't scratch the itch. Like you, right now.

Not everybody likes trivia. They're the well-adjusted. They're the people who won't let a little thing like the names and order of First Ladies, or the literal meaning of the word *yuan*, or the particulars of New York City's pneumatic mail service stand in the way of their peace of mind. I envy them, I envy you, every day.

I won't torture you very long. Just until we get to the university, a center of learning, after all.

■ ■ ■

The wind, Q. Hold my hand—.

Question two: Science. Ready?

Chinook, mistral, haboob, williwaw, sirocco, and Santa Ana are all names for different kinds of what phenomenon—?

The goofy smile gives you away. Total, happy unknowing. Next.

■ ■ ■

Thinking, thinking—.

■ ■ ■

American History. You're tall, Q, but you're not quite Abe Lincoln. Not yet.

Everybody knows Lincoln was the tallest president.

Who was second tallest? Or, if you don't like that one, who was the shortest president?

I'm not so sure I want to be tall. Short people live longer than tall people. I think life insurance companies charge higher premiums if you're higher off the ground, but I could be making that up. For sure, without their wealth and health care, Norwegians would die younger than the Sherpa, not counting avalanches, K2, and falling a thousand feet through a crevasse. Maybe. I don't know. I'm guessing.

You look nervous. I'm not saying you'll die young, Q. I'm—. Listen. It's just you might live longer if you were a fisherman from Okinawa instead of a linebacker from the United States.

Believe me. I want you around my whole life, but that's unlikely. Sorry. Unless my Chimaera kills me young, I'm short enough to live to a hundred.

■ ■ ■

I can see the clock tower and quad. I'm so tired.

We need a question—. Literature. Books. Something about books—. .

You read *Harry Potter*. Of course you did. All seven? Just nod.

I think our whole generation's read it. Everybody. But J. K. Rowling is not the best-selling woman of all time. Not by a lot. What woman—she's dead now, but not murdered—has sold the most books?

—?—

Here's another hint, in case you missed the first. My mother loves her.

—?—

Just as I thought.

■ ■ ■

In some book I read, the author described the sound of cars on wet pavement: like eggs frying in a pan. I can't remember who wrote it. Pretty good, right?

We have time, lucky you, for a couple more questions.

Let's try—Family History.

My grandmother—my father's mother, Gloria Fitzgerald, née Luz—suffered her whole life. I don't know how often, but at least once, if not a hundred times, she received shock treatment. Name one psychiatric illness this therapy was, and is, used to treat.

I think you'd get this right if I let you answer.

My grandmother never went very long before her mind

would give out. *Splat, boom, pishh.* A scream or a whimper or a long howl. In tears or silence. She disappeared before I was born. My father told me she got on a plane without telling anyone where she was going, one way.

Good-bye, Gloria.

■ ■ ■

We're kind of wet, but it's the last question. The subject is Astrology.

We're exactly between our birthdays today. I was born the end of July. You were born mid-December. According to our sun signs, are we compatible?

—?—

Please don't tell me you have to think about this.

—??—

You're going to break my heart now? Because of trivia? Because I said you might die young? Are we compatible or not?

All I could do was smile and nod.

The rain on our faces.

■ ■ ■ ■ ■ ■ ■

We landed inside Ford Hall, out of the rain. My head was
nearly bursting. At some point, I'd have to Google the answers
to Nest's questions: Harry Styles from the boy band; the names
of winds; Lyndon Johnson and James Madison; Dame Agatha
Christie; and electroconvulsive therapy, ECT, was used to treat
severe depression, catatonia, schizophrenia, and mania.

■ ■ ■

We can watch the weather from here. It's only a shower.
Enough to wet our faces and hands half cold, and to make
the ends of our shoes dark, and. Then it ends. Then comes
the beautiful light after the sun smashes through the
clouds. Your eyes are the color of that light ten minutes
from now.

I want the rest of this walk with you—I want everything to happen—in dry, gold air. I have promises to keep,
and miles to go before I sleep.

■ ■ ■

Yeah, I don't think I'll go to college. Why would I want to
waste what sanity I have left in classrooms? As it is, I'm
pretty good at reading and learning on my own.

I've always liked the tile floors in this old hall, though. My father, the professor: I've been coming here, trying doors and kicking back in these ancient armchairs, my whole life. I've imagined living inside the stained-glass windows and in the giant clock fifty feet over our heads, and. The forests carved into columns: bears and birds; caterpillars, millipedes, and beetles; vines and mice and owls. A fox or two.

Inside one of these columns, a woman reads novels and nibbles on sticks. In another column, a scrimshander sings to his ivory and bones every song that has ever made it into the world, even the songs the earth sings, the eerie songs that come up through oceans and animals and the miles of rock. The quartz and iron songs. The river and maple and snake—.

Whatever. Let me have my ideas.

A long time ago, one of the university presidents kept a pair of peacocks—.

Oh God. Peacocks. I can't get started on peacocks, Q. I can talk for a day just about peacocks. Believe me.

What do you think? Should I use up the rest of my mind in a university? Right here, in the middle of the mosaic, oak, and stone? There's still chalk and paper, right? For those of us who are old-fashioned? Maybe?

We're standing where the school is best. It weighs the most right here. It smells like ninety-nine percent perspiration and one percent inspiration, and you can hear the peacocks calling.

■ ■ ■

Time for Darwin—.

Survival of the fittest and natural selection: adapt or die. It's cruel, but.

Am I fit for survival? If I end up all Chimaera, if I bend over to tie my shoe and stand up completely insane—that fast—and if I'm locked up forever in an asylum, die there, then I will not have adapted to the world. Nobody could call me fit for anything. Nest Fitzgerald would be worthless, evolutionarily speaking.

"We can understand why—." I can quote Darwin, too: "We can understand why, when a species has once disappeared, it never reappears. . . . For the link of generation has been broken."

What dies, stays dead. And it's better off gone, since it didn't earn its place in the world. Or it gave up its place—slow, slow, slow, over a long time—to something better.

But what if my Chimaera lets me survive everything? What if she helps me climb up into the world?

What if I go to clown college and become a very successful mime? Or what if I make something of myself, whether or not I go to college? What if I end up like my grandmother Gloria, wandering in and out of her mind, but a mother? What if I die at one hundred, as I hope, a grandmother and great-grandmother and great-great-grandmother, even if my trick mind tricks me forever? I'm named for two very fit women who lived a thousand years ago. Will I give birth, like my namesakes, to royalty and generations? Will I pass on my Chimaera to heroes and heroines? Will the world owe its survival, at least a little of it, to a mind that has feathers and claws and trouble sleeping?

How can I let myself die if this is even a tiny bit possible?

On the other hand, why would I give birth to a fourth generation of Angers?

■ ■ ■

You remember I thought of Lincoln? Trivia: Lincoln and Darwin were both born on February 12, 1809. What a year, right? Napoleon was conquering Europe, and Lincoln and Darwin were born on the same day. Two hundred plus years later, the whole world's at war and still arguing race, slavery, and evolution.

When Darwin was a teenager, sixteen or something, his father got on him: "You care for nothing but shooting, dogs, and rat-catching, and you will be a disgrace to yourself and all your family." Ten years later, Darwin returned home to England from a five-year voyage around the world on the H.M.S. *Beagle*. He was twenty-six, twenty-seven years old, a naturalist with ten million notes and observations from his long trip, carrying around a huge baby of an idea. It took him decades to work it all out in his head, to raise the baby. Darwin was fifty when he published *The Origin of Species*, and he changed the world.

Let me take out Darwin. Look, just listen to this one thing from the very end of *Origin*.

"It is interesting to contemplate a tangled bank, clothed with many plants of many kinds, with birds singing on the bushes, with various insects flitting about, and with worms crawling through the damp earth, and to reflect that these elaborately constructed forms . . . have all been produced by laws acting around us. . . . Thus, from the war of nature, from famine and death, the most exalted object which we are capable of conceiving, namely, the production of the higher animals, directly follows. There is grandeur in this view of life . . . having been originally breathed by the Creator into a few forms or into one; and that, whilst this planet has gone circling on according to the fixed law of gravity, from so simple a beginning endless forms most beautiful and most wonderful have been, and are being evolved."

"You see?" Darwin says. "Life is huge and beautiful. But what God or whatever started with, the few and simple, became many and complicated. Creatures have come and gone and. Everything, absolutely everything is evolving. Even humans. We're evolving, getting closer and closer all the time to perfection."

Maybe perfection, even in me, even with my Chimaera. Maybe.

Darwin didn't count on us humans killing absolutely everything that lives and breathes. We love to murder. It's awful, but Darwin would have shrugged his shoulders. Far as he's concerned, something better than us might come along. Except, when the time comes, the sun will die. Darwin didn't count on this either. All of it will be over. Da Vinci and Hitler, the Koran and the Bible, scientists and antiscientists, Minotaur and Chimaera, all

the life before and after us, everything, all memory, the
two of us, gone.

■ ■ ■

Nest's mind bubbles and steams and swirls. Primordial soup,
and all sorts of creatures walk up out of her brain on their
fins, which become feet. Listening to Nest is only as tiring as
pretending to witness the start of the world.

■ ■ ■

Let's walk, Q. The rain's done. I have to walk so I won't
go to sleep.

Wait. The cold; watching the rain: I have to go before
we go.

Bathrooms are down the hall. They're next to each
other, Men's and Women's.

Do you know Morse code?

—?—

If you knew Morse, I could knock-talk, dots and dashes,
during the long separation.

MILE FIVE

I have everything I want to share with you up here, Q, in my head. Or in my heart. Quotes, you know. And poems, some whole poems. For today—.

We're almost to the bridge. And your eyes are lighting the world.

You're more beautiful than I am. You're rare. But I have a Chimaera. She's hiding from you, but she's in me, watching, and she makes me even more rare.

■ ■ ■

Almost always, on these forever walks, I cross the bridge. I like the graffiti, especially the tags painted in the places that look impossible to reach any normal way. I mean—.

Three friends climb and climb up past where everybody else wouldn't dare. No doubt or fear. You can see the guy with the paint, upside down, his friends holding his ankles. Or he rappels. Suction cups, maybe. It's much easier to believe he hovers like a hummingbird, his wings flapping a hundred beats a second. And when he's done, he collapses, totally exhausted. He falls straight down into the river, a finished angel, like Icarus with a can of paint, useless wings. He has to fight for life. But he left his mark, and that's what matters.

When I walk over the bridge, I stand in the middle, every time, and imagine what the world looked like before the city came. Hundreds of years ago, the land was forest and hills and cliffs and the river that cuts everything into this side and that side.

You'll see. You'll stop breathing for a second when you see how beautiful it all was. The forest that stopped only for the river and the sky, and finally the ocean. The noisy quiet, and the whole living world that never once asked itself, "What did I do that for? What was I thinking?"

■ ■ ■

This is the craziest thing about the bridge. No matter how you get here, you never see it coming. A couple lefts, a right, straight a few blocks, another left, and *wham*. There it is. Right now. Over our heads. So tall and.

Metal.

I always discover it, every time, as if it never existed before I thought it up.

■ ■ ■

And the first step every time feels the same way. The road vibrates and hums. The vibration goes through your body. For a second you have to wonder if you're doing the right thing, taking a bridge by foot over the water. There's no other way, though, that isn't scary. You can't swim the river. The ferry vibrates and hums, too. The train swings and screeches and slows down as if the tracks have to be crossed really gently or they'll snap. There's no way to get from here to there, one side to the other, without knowing it. You're awake and afraid.

"On Friday noon, July the twentieth, 1714, the finest bridge in all Peru broke and precipitated five travelers into the gulf below."

It doesn't matter how many times I take the bridge, I'm afraid it's going to crack and break. Bridges sometimes do that. And when I'm walking, a truck comes and the road and bridge shake a little wild. Or the train comes over and it makes such incredible noise. But I hold on to the steel, and I close my eyes, and I wait. I think, "This isn't the last day of my life."

◼ ◼ ◼

Never touched by decay
The bridge of Nagara's
Bridge pillars
Endure and so
Will you, I'd say.

◼ ◼ ◼

I have some poetry in me, Q, even ancient Japanese lines, poetry memorized over the years during the long nights when my candle burned at both ends and in the middle.

I'm not sure poems are all that good for me, since my imagination takes off, but.

Poetry finds me. I can't give up the beauty.

I know why I don't bother with Snapchat and Tumblr and fandoms and Instagram and GatherIt and FireFly and everything else I'm supposed to enjoy. What if this is our last day on earth?

Hashtag: Exit.

The word *hashtag* is now in the Oxford English Dictionary, by the way. Use it the next time you play Scrabble.

But what if this is our last day on earth? An undiscovered meteor comes screaming through the sky, and. Good as gone. Hashtag: Duck. Hashtag: Infinitewinter.

It's not pessimistic. I'm saying our last day is the first day of forever.

It matters what we do. Pretty much everything matters—.

"One ought, every day at least, to hear a little song, read a good poem, see a fine picture, and if it were possible, to speak a few reasonable words."

Everything matters. Like saying one thing that isn't completely stupid. Or reciting a poem from memory.

■ ■ ■

I feel like I'm yelling over the traffic and the voices of the bridge. I need my own voice to go the distance, for all the miles I have to talk to you—.

There's everything still on the other side of the bridge. So, I'm going to shut up.

We'll stop at the middle. We'll stand over the forests that aren't there.

■ ■ ■ ■ ■ ■ ■

We walked in the noise of the bridge toward its center. Tiny Nest on the inside of the walkway, me on the outside. I wanted to protect her from the traffic and any splashing from tires crashing through the long puddles.

I was remembering a time a year before, when I visited Nest's home uninvited. Nest hadn't been to school in two weeks, and I worried she'd be lost when she got back. Nest always had to play catch up, it seemed, and she always fought through. She did better than anyone ever could expect. Sometimes, she would submit brilliant essays or ace exams after her long absences; sometimes she would scrape by. Wildly inconsistent, I guess you could say.

Nest was gone two weeks, and I wanted to bring her my notes and assignments, all my work, anything to help. We were in a few classes together, but we almost never spoke. One of our quiet phases. We'd smile, though, never shyly, knowingly maybe. We were silent with each other. I can't claim to understand. Like I've said, I was waiting.

I went to the house after school, and Nest's mother answered the door. Nest is a girl exactly split between her mother and father. She has her mother's eyes and mouth, but what must be her father's nose and skin. Sometimes we see such people, who look as if their parents picked what they thought would work best and stitched it together into a child.

"Oh, hello." Nest's mother spoke in a way that made you think you could barely hear her, but you knew exactly what she'd said. Her voice not so much a whisper, but—. I don't have Nest's gift of words. I have my own gifts, and those gifts are in numbers. "Isaac," she said. "Or should I call you Q?"

"I'll answer to both," I said.

"Q is how Nest thinks of you, so I'll keep to your given name. Isaac, I'm Martha Fitzgerald. We've never actually met, but I've seen you grow up. Thirteen to now. It must have been tiring, all the height." She laughed. "Nest and I never went through that kind of exhaustion for the sake of height."

"I guess it was tiring, I don't remember."

"Your mother would, I'm sure." She smiled a second before

her face became serious. "I'm not wanting to be rude, Isaac, not inviting you in right off. Nest is camped in the living room, and I should ask if she would like a visitor. Would you wait a moment, please?"

"It's all right, Mrs. Fitzgerald." I took off my backpack and unzipped it. "I wasn't invited. I just have some schoolwork I'd like to leave for Nest. Don't bother her."

I handed Nest's mother a fat folder, and she took it with a smile. "And you're kind, too. Give me a second with Nest, all right?"

I nodded, and Nest's mother disappeared inside. I tried not to look through the blinds from the porch, but I couldn't help myself. The light was dim. I could make Nest out, lying under a blanket with her arm over her eyes. Her hand clenched into a fist. I saw her mother approach with the folder and begin to speak. At first, Nest didn't move. Then, she dropped her arm and propped herself up on her elbow. She turned her head and looked right out to me. Maybe she smiled, a flicker, but she shook her head. Slowly, so slowly, as if it might have hurt her to move any more. For all the world, I could imagine a goat, with its split eye and tapering beard, staring out after me from behind Nest's back.

When Nest's mother returned to the door, she came with a glass of water and a smile. "You must be a little thirsty," she said, mild as milk. "I'm sorry. Nest said no to the visit. Thank you for your generosity, Isaac. I'm sure you'll see Nest soon enough."

When Nest returned to school, she didn't come to me, and I didn't say anything. We smiled in class before we sat, and I thought she looked healthy. No sign of trouble having gone on in her body and mind.

Nest.

It's easy enough to wonder what all I've made up in these days I've written this out, as Nest lies somewhere in her own Between. Life, death, and the horizon line. How could I remember everything Nest said or everything I thought? Sometimes I sound like Nest and Nest sounds like me. Nothing of this can be perfect.

I can tell you only that I've repeated to myself this day we walked. I've relived this day, rebuilt it again and again.

It's a bridge of sorts, this walk, connecting one person who suffers from inside, in her mind, to one who doesn't. Nest has all her humor and observation and thought and knowledge, but I can't ever forget—especially now, with her face bruised and shut against everything alive, her broken body so close to nothing-more—she lives all the time near agony.

■ ■ ■

We came to the middle of the bridge that crosses a river into
the deep city. Nest leaned over the railing and stared down.
  Then:

  Flood-tide below me! I see you face to face!
  Clouds of the west—sun there half an hour
    high—I see you also face to face.

  That's from "Crossing Brooklyn Ferry" by Walt Whit-
man. It has a lot of words and is beautifully complicated.
I don't want you to get lost in what I say, Q. I want you to
follow me everywhere, and I know you can.
  I want poems for you that would be like songs, songs
to remind you where we stood.
  The arch is highest here, and we're exactly between
the towers.
  Look. Look at everything. Right now, watch the trees
and try to imagine yourself down there, in the never-
ending woods.

                    ■ ■ ■

Nest had built a forest around me in the middle of the bridge.
It was a forest of all her thoughts and feelings. The trees,

thorns, and wild vines. Almost impenetrable except for stars, animals, and sun spears. It was quiet and loud at the same time, like all forests. She surrounded me.

She stood next to me, shivering, holding her damp flannel at her throat. The breeze turned her lips purple-blue. I couldn't be sure I would ever get back to the forest Nest had made once I left it, but I wasn't at all sure I would ever leave it, no matter where I went, or how far from her.

I guess you can get lost in the city, in the forest of buildings, but not for long. You can never really get lost in a city or on an island. You have to pick a direction and walk. Or you can stand on a corner and cry until someone comes to help you. Draws you a map on the palm of your hand and.

In a city, you'll never be eaten alive or hear a tree explode in the cold.

Is this what happens in extreme winter? The sap running through a tree freezes and bursts the wood? A tree dying in this way would make a sound like a gunshot, or a cannon. The tree falls. But who would be there to hear it?

I leaned over the cable and guardrails, and I had the strange feeling of wanting to jump. Maybe this is what it feels like to be Nest.

Be careful, Q. Legs have their own mind, and they say, *Jump.*

If you jump, there would be nothing at all for me to hear, not even your body hitting the water—silence; only the image, the tiny clap of white visible from the bridge. What would you leave behind? Nothing. Not even graffiti.

Don't jump, Q. You'd miss me every day you were dead.

We finished the bridge in silence. Once Nest and I got past the graffiti on the towers, we could see the first traffic lights up the crosstown avenue. It seemed like a thousand stoplights and traffic to the horizon. The heart of the city.

MILE SIX

Just over the bridge comes the part of the city where everything necessary gets done. Garages, printers, and fabricators; food distributors and car parts. Wholesale/retail. People here cut glass and aluminum and plastic and tile and stone. But there is also the memory of work, and abandoned warehouses. The blocks are long and lonely.

Those giant, dead slaughterhouses, Q, right there, the city council and a developer want to make condos out of them. There must still be blood on the walls or in the cracks of the walls, and on the floors and ceilings. Who would buy a million-dollar condo in a slaughterhouse? I couldn't sleep with all the sweaty, bleeding ghost-cows crying and bellowing. How could anyone sleep?

■ ■ ■

I've had dreams about you, Q.

A square, white room, pretty big, twenty by twenty, and its ceiling is the sky, that close and endless. In the center of the room, there's a wood table and two chairs facing each other. I sit in one of the chairs. I'm in a gown, a wedding gown, made from ice, its train swept around and around my feet, hiding them. I have a crown, too, of leaves—maybe eucalyptus—but the leaves are frozen, iced over. My skin's pale, and my lips are blue.

I wait with my eyes closed and my hands on the table until I feel a presence in the second chair. I'm afraid to open my eyes. What if someone other than you has sat down?

I have to open my eyes. But I'm scared. I have to tell myself, "Open, open, open—"

And there you are. You.

I'm already crying. It feels like this is the first time

we've seen each other in a very long time, two or three times as long as we've been on the planet.

You nod. Or you drop your chin, simpler than a nod— not as, I don't know, confident.

I reach across the table, and you take my hands. Not a word. Half a minute this way, maybe, maybe half a minute or a thousand years, until I let go.

You push back your chair and stand.

"I'll wait outside," you say. "This room has to collapse sometime, Nest, and that dress will have to melt."

■ ■ ■

That's the most vivid dream. But I've had a repeating dream where we're chasing each other in the city: this city, but not this city. We're running through buildings and over rooftops and in the train tunnels. We find doors in the tunnels and in stations, doors nobody knows or remembers even exist. Doors that lead to blocked staircases, or stairs that go up into hotels. We're running to each other, looking for each other, but we're also running away from each other. We want to find each other, but we don't want to be found.

It's a paradox. And paradoxes are hard to live with.

There's a paradox this reminds me of. An ancient Greek came up with it. If we say, *Let's walk halfway to each other, and then halfway, and then halfway,* we will never meet because we're forever going only halfway. But we know we can get to each other. It can kind of make you crazy.

In my dreamworld, we are always exactly as far from each other as we are close. It's almost a nightmare. The perfect nightmare. I always start out laughing with the chase and end up crying. I want to find you and I want to be found, but it seems impossible.

<blockquote>

You, Beloved, who are all

the gardens I have ever gazed at,

longing. An open window

in a country house—, and you almost

stepped out, pensive, to meet me. Streets

    that I chanced upon,—

you had just walked down them and vanished.

And sometimes, in a shop, the mirrors

were still dizzy with your presence and,

    startled, gave back

my too-sudden image. Who knows? perhaps

    the same

</blockquote>

bird echoed through both of us

yesterday, separate, in the evening . . .

That's Rilke. It's another part of a poem, "You who never arrived."

Maybe one day I'll have that dream, nightmare, and we'll bump into each other. We'll back into each other in a hotel lobby. Or we'll come around a corner and crash. Or we'll cross the subway tracks between platforms, past the third rails, and meet in the middle and hold on to each other tight enough to become one person, as two trains whizz by us, so close, in opposite directions. Our hair and clothes whipping up, nearly torn from us in the wind.

■ ■ ■

Dreaming.

I want to lie down with you and stare at the sky. I don't care if anyone watches us. Don't you ever want to lie down right where you're standing—?

■ ■ ■

A dog trotted out of an alley, or from a shadow, or from be-
hind a Dumpster. I don't really know. Maybe she stepped out
of a seam in the air. A mangy, hungry dog, skinny and fat and
her head low.

    "Hello," Nest said. Then:

You're a pregnant girl. Dirty, but I like your white socks
and different-color eyes.

Nest crouched down with her hand out, but the stray didn't
even bother to sniff. She knew Nest had a good heart and
crawled under her hand and collapsed between her knees.

Sweet, hungry girl.

    Q?

I'm terrified of dogs. I had a dream when I was a young
boy, or maybe it happened: a German shepherd barking and
barking and barking at me while I sat at the top of a play-
ground slide. I couldn't slide down: I would go straight into
the dog's mouth. I couldn't take the ladder: the dog would run
around and jump and pull me down and eat me alive. I cried,
I wailed at the top of the slide. My memory ends right there.

Wait—. Are you afraid of dogs? That will have to change. Come here.

I could see the dog was starving for love and food.

Put your hand on her, Q. You can feel the puppies.

I couldn't touch Nest, but I could touch the forlorn dog and be a little closer.

The stray whimpered a little and panted. This had to be pleasure.

Can you imagine her life? She's hungry. She's in terrible shape.

You see the fleas? She's covered.

I remembered once giving a six-inch Yorkshire terrier on a leash about ten feet of room. I walked way out into the street to make sure I wouldn't get bitten. But there I was with Nest, fearless, kneeling at the head of a wild and filthy dog, a crushed and masterless dog. My hand might have been an acre from Nest's. Even so, something made me think I was comforting her through the stray.

Are you crying? Q—? I can't tell.

I don't know if I was crying. Maybe. So what?

This mama dog lives about as low to the ground as possible, lower than a worm. She'll be dead soon. I can't imagine she'll live through winter. And all her puppies will die.

Yes, so I cried. I had to ask myself, And you, Nest, will you live through winter? Will you live a long life?

■ ■ ■

The dog followed us.

She walked and jogged behind. She stopped when we stopped. She kept close to the walls of the long warehouses. Those blocks after the bridge take forever to walk. You feel as if you're crossing an endless plain. And the dog followed.

Nest hardly said a word the whole time. A note about the abandoned warehouses and the riverfront and the old weedy train tracks that ran along the cliffs, but I don't remember. Nest seemed defeated by the dog's sadness. Finally, she turned to the dog.

And the dog came close.

Nest sat down on the concrete and smoothed the stray's belly and rubbed her ears. She might have been talking with the dog, but I didn't hear any of it. The traffic, a couple people walking by, but nothing of the conversation right in front of me.

Nest and the dog, communing.

I can't say that stray cured me of my fear. But it's true I decided I wanted someday to have a puppy of my own, a little life that grows into a big life. I wanted that dog to be named Helen.

What explains a dog's knowledge?

Nest stood up and turned to me. She shrugged. "Let's walk."

The dog didn't even hesitate. She walked off in the other direction without another word. Her belly of unborn puppies swung heavy under her bony back.

The knobs of her hips.

▦ ▦ ▦

I made my peace with her. She's probably the tenth dog I've met on these walks. The first was with my father. A stray he had seen on his walks as the Minotaur. That mutt had long blue dreadlocks.

I'm serious. The dog was blue. So whatever mix makes blue hair—.

I don't know.

He came to us, the dog, head high and smiling, at the start of an alley. My father reached down, and the dog licked his hand.

"He's not afraid of me," my father said. "Someone, somewhere, takes care of him, I think. He's fed, but he's always outside."

"Does he have a name?" I said.

"I don't know." My father smoothed the dog's ears, and I scratched the dog's back.

"Let's name him," I said.

"You can," my dad said. "I'm sure he won't mind."

It took me less than a second to come up with a name. "Matthew."

"Matt or Matthew?"

"Matthew," I said.

Matthew sneezed and shook his head.

"Quite suitable," my father said. "A couple times I've found him, Matthew, lying not too far away from me when I finally—. I wake up from my Angers, and he's there. It's strange. I calm down, and I realize where I am, and he's wagging."

The dog trotted away suddenly, like he'd heard his true name past our hearing. He disappeared into the alley.

"I'm glad Matthew keeps you company," I said. I was ten, I guess. Or nine. Or eleven. "Maybe he protects you."

"Maybe." My dad held my hand, and we walked.

"Maybe he feels bad for you."

"Undoubtedly." My father laughed. "What does it say about a man when a dog pities him? He was even smiling just then as if he'd never seen me look better."

▓ ▓ ▓

We met Matthew in the morning, but my father took me out mostly after dark, when I couldn't sleep. Only one time that I can remember right now did someone get upset with him enough to say something.

"What kind of father are you, keeping a kid up at night? Late as this."

But how many times did people think it? A man and a young girl, all times of night, walking the streets. My father and I could walk pretty far, and sometimes we ended up in some sketchy neighborhoods. Not the worst. Only bad enough.

"Hey, buddy, why isn't your kid at home in bed?"

"Insomnia, Officer. Nightmares."

"Hers or yours?"

"Hers."

"And so you thought you'd comfort her by taking in the sights and sounds of this part of our great city?"

"We were walking. I didn't even really think about it. I want her to know the world, and I don't want her to fear it."

"Uh-huh. A little fear's not a bad thing, bud. Some places shouldn't be, I guess, frequented."

"No, sir. You're right."

"Uh-huh." Then, turning to me: "You sleepy, hon?"

I nodded. I wasn't thinking.

The cop looked sideways at my father.

"No," I said. I looked at the cop, then my dad. "No. I'm not tired. Really. We're just walking."

The officer frowned all the way down his uniform at me.

"Uh-huh. If you don't mind, I think I'll take you two home."

■ ■ ■

This never happened. But it could have. Maybe it even should have. My father would take me to the bathroom in bars, nightclubs, all-night joints. He'd get me a glass of water or pretzels or nuts. I'm not saying it's right. He doubted himself, for sure. He'd say, "Don't tell Mom where we go. It'll just upset her."

Then why?

My father didn't take me to the dead zones—to the Hill or to St. William or the Fort or. The neighborhoods where people starve and suffer and die. I think my father wanted me to see the places not even half as bad as all that where I couldn't ever go safely on my own after dark. You know where I mean. You could walk there, maybe. You're big and male; I'm little and female. You might never know what it's like to be afraid to walk down certain streets. Depends on where you travel, I guess.

You're safe almost everywhere, Q. Tall, strong, and white.

Leave it at that.

■ ■ ■

What if I told you you'd have to wait years to kiss me? Would you wait?

If I said, *Isaac, we're not allowed to see each other for five years. I'm going to travel around the world, here and there, north and south and east and west. Pray and garden at monasteries; work, dance, race camels; walk from Marrakesh to Cairo, and ride a bicycle from Tikal to Cuzco; take a river barge on the Mekong; sleep in a cave hotel in Cappadocia; and climb Kilimanjaro, Fuji, and Pike's Peak.* Would you wait?

Of course you would. Waiting doesn't mean you have to stop living. You can go about your business. Waiting means you have to live knowing the best has yet to come.

Waiting builds character.

And I might just make you wait.

Or not.

■ ■ ■

My mother waited for my father. Mostly. She talks Between about a guy named Cabot. I don't know if that's his first name or his last.

I don't mean the cowboy. My mother, wide-awake, told me about the cowboy when I asked her.

"Popp and Dye—." My grandparents: don't ask. "Popp and Dye always enjoyed a good church hoedown, a roaring square dance." Why are you laughing? My mother said, "Popp and Dye would take their kids, not the whole lot, but by twos. That cowboy was a friend of a friend of a friend. He seemed huge to me, out of a tall tale. Like Pecos Bill, who roped the wind."

What movie was it where some goofy guy tells his girlfriend, "You want the moon? Just say the word, and I'll throw a lasso around it and pull it down"?

No, Cabot was someone else, not a cowboy. I don't know much, except—.

I think he kept in touch with Martha after she married, even after she had me. Vladimir wouldn't let it get to him usually. But the Angers, the Minotaur: Cabot would come up, and the Minotaur would threaten to hunt him down.

Cabot's a simple enough story. A man who wanted a woman and suggested she might want to think about it. Think about it and think about it and think about it. He never really understood *No*. Although, it never occurred to me until this second how Cabot might have waited for my mother. Maybe he never married. Maybe love never left him.

Possible?

Anyway, he had pitched a tent in some part of my mother's heart. I don't mean Martha held him in reserve, just in case, or even gave him much thought, though I don't know. Cabot showed up Between, which means he was a truth of some kind. I wonder how many people keep someone tucked inside their imagination: the what-if, the maybe-now.

Would I do that to you? Would you do that to me? You've had girlfriends, Q. Maybe I'm the one you've held in reserve while kissing someone else.

All the waiting.

Or could one of those girls be here with us right now? Will one of them be living inside you ten or twenty years from this moment? How about when I lose my mind for good? Or when my Chimaera makes you run for cover? My Chimaera is more a warning than a punishment, but.

This is poisontalk. I can feel the Angers bubbling, right? I can feel my Chimaera waking her goat and serpent.

I have to breathe—.

My father went through this, the sneaky Angers.

Cabot: a man who lost—. Still.

▬ ▬ ▬

At this moment, Nest first showed a sign of cracking. I wanted to say something, I wanted to ease her mind, but I thought my voice might upset her even more. I learned helplessness. I learned love doesn't always penetrate distress. And I learned Nest could turn and fold on herself—like an oxbow in a river—from one minute to the next.

■ ■ ■

It's impossible to feel secure when you have a Minotaur inside of you, or a three-faced Chimaera. It's impossible to feel secure when you have Angers. It's impossible not to feel weak and unlovable and ugly when your mind rattles. You wait and wait for total madness or rejection. Both inevitable.

You, darling, will never know what this feels like. You won't really have to fear where you walk, and you won't really have to fear your mind or fear becoming—.

I wouldn't wish any of it on an enemy.

MILE SEVEN

Keep your eyes open. We have to find something for you to carry home. A memento, but also a promise. For a second, I thought we should pick up that sink we just passed, but that seems unfair. Too heavy, even for you. I figured maybe the old faucets, separate hot and cold, maybe we could take them off, and you could carry them—.

What do you think? Faucets?

— . . . —

No?

All right, but we'll find something. I'm kind of hoping

it'll be a stuffed owl. I don't know. Some kind of taxidermy. A fox, its snarl frozen for eternity.

—!—

This surprises you? How about a framed butterfly? Would that make you happy?

Or a bowling pin?

■ ■ ■

We have arrived. And we must go in.

This is my favorite hotel, the Miranda. It's not big, and it's kind of worn-out, but.

I think a Chinese investor bought it, which means it'll never be the same once it goes through renovations. I think it's one of the last residence hotels in the city. Someone we know—Achilles? No, Sean—has a great-grandmother who's lived here fifty-seven years. She's ninety-two, a widow, and she won't budge. Over all the years, that lady grew roots right down through the bedrock underground. The hotel's waiting for her to die.

I love this lounge. The woodwork, the panels, the art. I have this plan that when I'm old enough to drink, I'm going to visit every hotel lounge in the city, a tour of high and low culture. I'll start here, in one of the leather arm-chairs, drinking a Sloe Miranda, a drink invented by a bartender in 1963. Sloe gin, pepper, milk—.

I might be making that up. But it's a concoction of something strange. Maybe bat guano.

Whatever.

We're taking the stairs, big boy. This way—.

Be a gentleman and hold the door for me.

And up we go.

■ ■ ■

There are, I discovered, 228 hotels in this city. This doesn't count every place where you can stay, which might number into the thousands. Just hotels. Of the 228, 227 have an active lounge that serves booze. In 1909, a financier named Hogarth built the Hyacinth, named after his second wife. Hogarth, a Baptist, never drank, and the hotel still refuses to sell alcohol, though it does have one of the best juice bars in the world apparently. No martinis, but you can get cold-pressed almond milk all day long for about nine hundred pennies a glass.

Okay, what was I thinking? Just a couple more flights. The eighth floor.

For some reason, I thought taking the stairs would be good for us, wake us up a little. We'll take the elevator down.

First, I want to show you a door.

■ ■ ■

In May 1957, a man named Grayfield Justice took a room, number 802. He said he'd stay for a week, but a week turned into a month, and a month turned into two, and two into twelve. By October 1958, almost a year and a half after Justice took over the room, the hotel wondered what in fact was going on with 802. Mr. Justice had never been late with payment, but he also had never been seen coming or going. His bill, paid by cash, first daily, then monthly, simply appeared in an envelope under a potted lily kept fresh at the front desk. Visitors were never reported—Justice himself was invisible—but the money showed up. Justice never ordered room service, never asked for his laundry to be done, never called for housekeeping, and never called reception.

Finally, on October 7, 1958, the Miranda's day manager, a man named Firth, announced himself at 802. No answer.

"Mr. Justice?" Nothing. Firth knocked. "Mr. Grayfield Justice? Please open the door."

Firth turned to his assistant, McCarthy, who slid the master key into the lock.

The key didn't work.

Mr. Firth and Mr. McCarthy frowned at the door. The door right here. In front of us.

Firth spoke up. "Justice, if you're in there, open up. Otherwise, I will call the police." No answer. Firth tried the master key himself and got nowhere. He tried the knob, and—.

Nope.

Firth called the police. A quick investigation turned up nothing about Grayfield Justice, and why would it? As far as the constabulary could figure, no such man ever officially existed.

Firth and McCarthy accompanied a small force of the Five-O to this room.

The police knocked and then banged on the door.

Silence.

The police shouted; they hammered: nothing. They had no choice. One of the junior officers put his shoulder to the door and.

Empty. Clean. Not a smudge, not a thing out of place.

Room 802 felt a little cold, a few degrees low, but the window was open. It's not a crime to leave the window open, is it?

Firth nodded at McCarthy. "Would you close that, please?"

Simple enough: close a window. McCarthy, though, died trying.

■ ■ ■

Let's take the elevator back down. It'll take us longer than the stairs. It shakes and groans the whole time, like you're riding an old man's back, but it's part of the experience.

Don't you love the paper on the walls? The burgundy flowers and gold stems. This will all go, and the faux gas lamps, too. Who knows what money will do to this hotel? I'm sure it will be swanky. It'll have a lounge with metal chairs and a glass bar and cool blue lighting. The rooms will have every luxury. Just what you want out of a woman named Miranda. A gorgeous, perfect, luscious wonder at five hundred a night.

But what will they do about room 802?

■ ■ ■

I never think about how dimly lit the Miranda is until I'm back outside. It really is almost dark in there. That sun. Maybe if the police, Firth, and McCarthy had had more light, something to let them see deeper into the room, a light as bright as the sun, then McCarthy wouldn't have died. Maybe, but unlikely. No amount of light can let you see through a wall.

At first, the four policemen and Firth couldn't move. Fully five seconds went by without anybody doing anything. They simply couldn't understand how McCarthy had fallen out of the window, or where the dog had come from.

Once the dog's barking broke through the five thick skulls, everything changed. The junior officer with the broad shoulders shot the dog, and, finally, the men could think. Firth looked out the window at McCarthy, eight floors down and broken in the alley. A senior officer called for backup, and two more officers checked the bathroom.

In the bathroom, there were dog bowls and an open cage. And in the bathtub, behind the curtain, ten stacked black suitcases. In eight of the suitcases, investigators found more than nine hundred thousand dollars. The last two held four neatly wrapped human heads.

* * *

This city, like every city, has its unsolved mysteries, and the mystery of room 802 at the Miranda went unsolved. No one named Grayfield Justice ever appeared. No one found the source of the money. The heads went unidentified. And the dog's keeper—tipped off?—never showed up. Absolutely no one could figure out how a healthy, giant dog could be kept hidden in a residence hotel.

And what about housekeeping? Were they paid to stay away? Or were they bored visiting a room they never needed to clean? Wouldn't housekeeping have discovered the changed lock? How long ago had the lock been changed?

Justice had arranged with the head housekeeper never to send anyone to 802. She claimed she accepted the scheme over the phone and admitted to receiving a cash payment in an envelope tucked inside a newspaper left for her weekly. She was no help, and it didn't matter anyway.

The Miranda never used 802 again. There have been claims: a man screaming and the sound of a body hitting pavement, a black dog loping down the hall. The dog the police killed was white, but. People have heard a dog barking and panting, scratching at the wall, even howling. Standard paranormal activity. Nothing special.

■ ■ ■

Oh. My. God.

String art. I think it's one of Nelson's ships. It's beautiful and totally ridiculous.

It's just sitting here—.

People are nuts. Giving away treasures. You want to carry that home for us?

—?—

What? The velvet and the string, all the colors of midnight: you don't like it? A three-masted ship rolling on the high seas? What's not to love?

—?—

You don't know what you're looking for until you find it. So true.

But I think we'll regret leaving this behind. I'm serious, Q. If we don't see anything better, we're coming back for this. I swear. And if it's gone, you'll be sorry.

■ ■ ■

So, ants are the worst people. They're vicious, hungry for land, and they kill and plot to kill. Not much to like about ants.

On the floor of a Costa Rican rain forest, there lives an especially bloodthirsty species of ant. They are at war almost all their lives. And along the edges of the battlefield, a species of fly, the phorid, waits out the war between colonies while rubbing its skinny legs. When the flies see injured ants, they buzz on over, say a little prayer over the soldiers, and tear off their heads. Turns out ants don't have much of a brain, but they have muscles in their heads to work their massive pincer jaws, and they have nutrients important to fly health. Their heads are chunks of meat.

Go figure: ant heads are delicious. The phorids eat and drink. Then, as if that weren't enough, the flies go ahead and lay eggs in the skull and corpse. Sometimes, up to eight flies will lay their eggs in one ant.

The man who told me this was a friend of my father's, an entomologist named Dr. M—I won't tell you his full name. He whispered the story of the ants and flies to me just after he kissed me. I was fifteen.

I didn't know what else to do, so I said to him, "Will one of those flies attack an uninjured ant?"

Dr. M pushed my hair off my cheek and hooked it around my ear. He kissed my forehead.

"Never," he whispered and kissed my ear. "If you put an ant and a fly in a room together to sort things out, the ant would win every time. The fly, Nest, wouldn't survive ten seconds."

■ ■ ■

I'm pretty sure Dr. M is the reason my father doesn't talk directly to me anymore. Not because I did anything to ruin their friendship. Dr. M did that all on his own.

He used to come to dinner once, sometimes twice a week. He even stayed for a little while at our house, but I was really young then. He and my father were the best of friends, roommates once, all that jazz. Dr. M married and divorced twice in less than six years. He lost three houses. He was miserable at life, and miserable at getting along with everyone except my dad. My mom, I don't think, ever liked him, which is saying something. He flirted terribly with her, awkwardly, which my dad swallowed. But he would also say awful things at dinner, rude things, and curse, and my mother finds poor behavior at the table unforgiveable. Let that be a warning to you.

I grew up with Dr. M coming and going, and he—. I got used to hearing about this insect and that. One moth and another beetle, and the soap opera of the beehive. He kept his hands to himself.

I know, this is all summary, not a lot of detail, but I'm trying to get somewhere without getting distracted. The night he kissed me.

The whole event couldn't have been more than two minutes, and I don't, to this day, know how it could have happened. I think this is one of the frightening things about certain crimes: they can happen so fast. You can slowly build a crime, like Grayfield Justice in the Miranda, or you can start and end it in a breath. No one will ever be able to explain to me how I ended up behind the bathroom door with Dr. M. And no one will ever be able to explain to me how I ended up back in the hall, kissed for the first time by a man, the prickles of his mustache still in my nose, scared and confused and less than ten feet from my mother and father. Where does a girl find a Chimaera when she needs one?

■ ■ ■

And why are baby strollers so huge? Babies are small, but their vehicles—. It's totally stupid. Did you see that woman with a double stroller trying to get into the coffee shop? She had to have both doors opened. I'm sure she took up the entire counter. She could barely steer it.

Money buys room. Money buys freedom from the un- desirables always pressing in. Money buys strollers the size of baby elephants. And the tires? That stroller could cross the Outback, even if the mother pushing it dies trying.

But the mothers, I guess, would say, "Just look at everything we have to carry."

Really? It's a baby. You're not the supply train for an army regiment. You're not Hannibal crossing the Alps. Why do you have more than people who have smaller strollers, people who can't afford your stroller?

No wonder the terrorists hate us.

■ ■ ■

You see? I got distracted anyway.

After the bathroom kiss, I went back to the dinner table, and Dr. M, a minute later, took his seat at the oppo- site head of the table, across from my father.

"Dessert, yes, Martha?" Dr. M said.

"Of course," my mother said and disappeared into the kitchen.

"Well, it's really more like two desserts for me." Dr. M put his hand over mine and smiled at my father. Had he lost his mind completely?

I think my father felt like the police and Firth at the door of room 802. One second, McCarthy is headed to close a window; the next, he's falling eight stories to his death. A dog barking. And they simply don't know what to do. Complete silence and stillness until.

But my father didn't wake up. My mother had gone to put together dessert, and my father sat and blinked at his friend, not even toward me. The unthinkable had occurred, and my father rammed right into the end of his brain. He just couldn't add it up.

Dr. M pulled his hand away when my mother came in from the kitchen with a tray. She stood for a moment, watching all of us. She didn't know anything. How could she? Even so, my mom said, "Kenneth, it's time for you to go."

"Oh, Martha," M said. "Don't I get my tarts?"

"Here," my mother said and handed him the tray. "All for you. And nothing else."

Dr. Kenneth M ignored the dessert tray. He pushed out his chair and leaned on the end of the table. "Vladimir," he said, "you have everything. And I have nothing. But I've tasted what's yours."

■ ■ ■

My father had started talking to me less when my breasts started showing. I must have been eleven, sixth grade. He stopped holding me in his lap, and he never came into my bedroom alone. Did he spy on me through keyholes? Did he imagine himself in my bed, see himself with a pen in his hand, tinkering with a formula on my bare skin? How did he avoid an aneurysm, his brain exploding with impure thoughts? Red wire of lust connected to one terminal, yellow wire of conscience connected to the second terminal: the bomb set and ticking. Could that be possible? I loved him, and he loved me. My handsome father, with his Angers and Minotaur: couldn't he trust himself?

Of course he could. My father is good and decent, the best, even if he fell in love with a teenager named Martha when he was already a grown man. He and my mother are very much in love, and their story is pure.

No. My dad? He simply can't stand watching me get

older. He'll talk to me when I'm all growed up. He'll laugh with me and come back to me, take a walk with me, my father, when he can look me in the eye, as a man meets a woman. A woman with her own Angers and a Chimaera, a woman with her own life and body and destiny. This in-between, teenager thing? He wants no part of it. It makes him nervous.

Like my mother's Between sleep. My father can't stand anything that's not one thing or another. One reason I'm sure he hates his Minotaur: between man and bull. Let him be a man, or make him a bull forever. The torture of being both?

My father is afraid of me. And he worries about me, but he has no way to cope. My mind upsets him, I'm sure, since he doesn't want me caught between human and—.

He's afraid. For all sorts of reasons. And that's the way it is. He's abandoned me, but it won't be forever. He'll come back. I believe it.

And I miss him.

The night Dr. M kissed me and left our house for good, I lay in bed biting my hand and crying. I knew my father was gone from me. And I knew I'd have to deal with real men from then on. Dr. M only started the game. I went to sleep all sorts of upset; but at some point during the night, for the first time in almost four years, my dad came and sat on the edge of my bed, his hands clasped in his lap and his head low. Maybe he was calming down, trying to catch his breath after the outrage of the evening. Maybe he was thinking or gathering his strength. I almost couldn't believe he hadn't become the Minotaur after the whole mess and gone off to murder his old friend, Kenneth M.

But there he sat, silence and the blankets between us, while I pretended to sleep.

Then, as if he knew—of course he knew—he started counting backward, so quietly and gently.

"One hundred. Ninety-nine. Ninety-eight. Ninety-seven—."

Darkness.

■ ■ ■

Maneki-neko.

That would be good to take home, and it's not too heavy. Look at her. You know what breed of cat she is? A Japanese calico bobtail. They're all Japanese calico bobtails, all the *maneki-neko*, the waving cats. But she's not waving, she's beckoning. She's saying, "Come in, come in to our Laundromat and leave your dry cleaning."

This cat looks ceramic, not plastic. Don't you love the red collar and the gold bell?

Here's the problem. We're not allowed to steal anything. It's a found object we can take home. Not only is it wrong to steal, it's stupid to steal a good luck charm, since it will probably bring bad luck to the thief. Though, if you get away with stealing it in the first place, I guess it could be considered good luck after all—.

Another one of my moments. I'm sorry.

All I'm saying: this kitty belongs to this business; she's not ours. We didn't so much find it as catch it in the window. She's not sitting and waving, or beckoning, on the curb.

I'm still regretting the string art, but we'll keep going.

■ ■ ■

We have to—.

Check it out. From this corner, you can see the four tallest buildings this city has to offer. And they go in size order, shortest to tallest, right to left, starting with Locke and Bowles. Then the Eastman Building, Spectator Tower, and the Honey Building. On the day of the summer solstice every year, the sun comes up between Spectator and Honey and fills the whole thin street, east/west, with blinding orange light.

■ ■ ■

Is Dr. M the kind of man who should have his feet broken after he dies, so he can't walk back into the world as a ghost? Should his coffin be weighed down with extra stones?

Is he a criminal pedophile?

Dr. M might be a great entomologist—I don't know—but for sure he's a failure at real life, and he's angry and sad about it. Pedophile? I don't think so.

I've thought about this for two years. Dr. M is no Humbert Humbert, and I'm no Lolita. He kissed, if you could call it that, the fifteen-year-old daughter of his best friend behind the bathroom door and all but admitted it two minutes later, an action that in a strange way is exactly as safe as it is dangerous. He didn't shove his tongue in my mouth, and he didn't even touch me with his hands, except my hair. He whispered about phorid flies and ants at war, which was—.

Frightening for sure, but also desperate.

I'm not excusing him. He ruined me. He destroyed my mouth forever. I'll never have the first kiss I should have had.

And.

I haven't let anyone kiss me since Dr. M stole his. That's the truth. But you know this already. Of all the things people at school make fun of me for, what's the thing I hear the most? Not that I take drugs. Not that I'm weird or a nerd or totally crazy or everything a girl shouldn't be. Not for how I dress, or my infrequent school attendance.

I get made fun of most regularly for being, or seeming, asexual. Uninterested. Private. People tell me I don't look like I should be uninterested, whatever that means. They tell me I could be sexy. I'm not exactly ugly, they say, and I'm not stupid. I'm even funny. So why don't I go out? Why don't I see anybody, boy, girl, man, woman? Why don't I take selfies and fall in love with myself at least? What's my problem?

That's what I hear almost every day I show up at school: "What's your problem?"

But you know me. I do look: I look at you. And you look at me. You like how I walk, and you're dying to touch me. You're walking and walking, mile after mile with me. The bridge, the university, the cemetery, a homeless man, poetry, quotes, Darwin, rain, trivia; a pregnant, dying dog; the mysterious Miranda; Vladimir and Martha; the Minotaur and Chimaera, and. You're not allowed to speak. You killed a mouse. But through everything there's *koi no yokan*. Inevitable love.

■ ■ ■

This is it. Stop where you are. Even you can't resist. Maybe it isn't string art or taxidermy, but it's better than a figurine of a waving cat, and a sink and faucets. Someone's a genius. When have you ever seen a spaceship in a bottle?

And the *Millennium Falcon?*

Come on, now. I want it. We just have to find a new cork.

Are you kidding me—? No way. You can see Han Solo and Chewbacca in the cockpit.

Hi, Han. Hi, Chewie.

Wrap it in my flannel, Q. We've found gold.

MILE EIGHT

How can I recall everything?

I forgot, until right now, the first quote of the day, when we started out. From Henry David Thoreau, who loved his walks: "Methinks that the moment my legs begin to move, my thoughts begin to flow." It doesn't change the story, my forgetting to put that in. Nest was preparing me, nothing else. It only proves I won't remember in perfect order or include all that was seen, said, and done, no matter how hard I've tried.

Walking in the city: endless shops, restaurants, cafés, buildings, cars, buses, taxis, and all the people striding,

riding, running, and moving. A person can't remember every dress in a window, every necklace and ring; every man and woman down on their luck; every millionaire; every sculpture, poster, and mural; every busker strumming for coins. Did I mention the edition of cat haiku and a copy of The New Joy of Sex, *in hardcover, on the dollar table outside a bookshop? Or the dog walker with nine leashes attached to nine different dogs? Or the mannequin dressed in black, bent to resemble a cocked gun?*

You can't find the whole story of my half walk with Nest, because it doesn't exist. Or it does, but only in the memory of a god, or in the memory of the Fates, not in any human mind. Not even in Nest's.

And the whole story, every detail, would bore people enough to make them cry. Who wants to read about the five hundred times I checked the pimple behind my ear? Who wants to read about the dog poop on the curb, the spilled soda, the sun striking the windshield of a convertible?

■ ■ ■

Even now, in story time, we're still walking, Nest and I. We're walking, and Nest is talking. She's in her jeans and white tank. It's as warm as the day will get, maybe seventy. She's

moving as she walks, like I've said, her whole body, not in a
riot but in a dance.

We go street after street, light after light; we turn one way
and another.

This is one of my favorite shops: Ladyfinger. Where else
would I find a hand-painted tarot deck, hand-stitched
shoes, hand-knit scarves, hand-dyed denim, hand-tooled
leather journals, and hand-wrought bronze jewelry, none
of it affordable for a girl like me, in a space no bigger than
a closet?

I won't make you go in, but I love it.

We should have gone in. We should have dawdled and
laughed. I would've made a mental list of what Nest
wanted most, what I would have to save for and buy in a
thousand years.

Instead, we made it to the corner two blocks east in time
for a car that jumped the curb.

Maybe the talk of Dr. M poisoned Nest. Maybe her
tiredness started to catch up, the few hours talking to me,
entertaining me. But the wild car that never stopped, the
driver who might have killed us both, or a kid on a bike, or
a grandmother with her shopping, that was the last straw.

"Did he stop?" Nest bent over and moaned.

The close car—.

Nest shook her head, like a horse shaking off a fly. "Did he stop?"

She gnashed her teeth, and on that street corner, in the moment's commotion and among the mob, I could hear her molars creaking.

Nest hissed and snorted, and she retched over the curb.

Nest suffered. What could I do? I put my hand on her back, to soothe her and:

"Don't you touch me."

Chimaera.

I knew her voice. It had to be her voice: low, husky, and arctic.

"Don't you ever touch me." I couldn't see her faces. "And don't say a word. Don't let our Eleanor hear you. Don't add your pretty voice to all the noise, the engines and horns and shouting."

Then she stood.

What can I say? Nest and not-Nest. Horns and beard; muscle and mane; hood, fangs. Split hoof, split tongue, and six blue, stone eyes.

Smoke.

Behind the three faces, a dream of Nest.

"Be careful." The Chimaera stretched her goat's head to whisper in my ear: "The Angers."

I stood back.

Harelipped lion: "Are you afraid?"

I shrugged.

Smiling goat: "I'm not your enemy."

Silent, weaving snake.

Nest's Chimaera hardly ripples when she walks. Poised, I think you could call it. Only her restless serpent.

She crossed the street, and I followed.

"You should be afraid," the Chimaera said. "You live in a world where you can die on the street at any moment. The careless men who kill. The careless women who kill. The children who laugh and laugh, because the dying people look funny to them. What makes you so different, young man? What makes you worthy of our Eleanor? What makes you more than another? No answer? Nothing to say? Nothing but your gaping mouth and your fear—? Are you anything other than ugly? Are you beautiful? Are you not different for your patience and courage? Your kindness toward our Eleanor?"

The Chimaera stopped. She frowned at me, three ways: all sadness. "I'm not supposed to be here. Eleanor hoped and hoped you wouldn't meet me, wouldn't see my heads and fire, but then the car and fear and tiredness and memory and longing and—."

The Chimaera led me into a dark vestibule between a pizza parlor and a florist. I remember a black iron door and a brass lock.

"It's not supposed to be like this. I'm not wanted here."

The snake coiled, the goat buried her head in the lion's mane, and the lion slid to the concrete.

■ ■ ■

"I feel sick to my stomach." Nest wiped her eyes and pushed back her hair. "I know what this means."

What could I do? What could I say?

"Please don't say anything. It had to happen sometime." She held her head and coughed. "Could you find me a ginger ale or water?"

The cup of water came from the pizza place. Nest was standing against the iron door when I got back.

"Thanks." She drank a little, and tried smiling at me.

She doesn't always stay long. Did she talk to you?

Of course she did. Couldn't have been much, though. We didn't go very far.

That car. We live in a world where anyone could die

on the street at any time. No one should die waiting to cross the street. No one should die on the curb.

We didn't. We might have, though, and some—.

I'm sorry, Q. I don't remember anything after the car. I saw a little girl's hand pressed up against the window. Did she even know what had happened? Was her father driving? I never remember what happens.

Did she hurt you, my Chimaera?

I guess that sounds like a stupid question. You're huge, but she's big, twice me. And I imagine she's much stronger, lion strong. And don't forget the chance of fire.

Nest finished the water and started to cry.

I can barely look at you. I'm so—.

And I can't imagine what you're feeling right now. You must really regret ever having taken this walk with me. If I were by myself, I'd have walked with my Chimaera until she finally left. Who knows? Maybe miles.

But what about us, you and me? We've gone too far to go separate ways. We'd have to take the same train, but different cars, or different times. Or one of us by bus, the other by.

I should make myself walk home, and you should

take the bus. Would you leave me here? I'd be all right. Perfectly fine. I'd just.

Would you leave me here—?

No. You wouldn't. There's a reason I chose you. As if I'd had a choice. I trust you. My Chimaera trusts you.

We've been through a lot on this walk, Q, which is why I.

I walk to live.

We have to walk to live. I can't stand here, crying, snotting, shivering, and.

I have to calm down. We have to keep going.

We're going somewhere, you know? Not a destination you can measure or photograph, but we're going to a place I've never been. You have to come with me. Only you.

■ ■ ■

Was I scared?

No. Not anymore.

Calm, sad, watchful. Amazed. Not afraid.

Nest worried for me. Even her Chimaera worried for me. And I worried for them. When you watch a girl lose herself to her beast, you have to wonder what it does to the girl.

The Chimaera usually stays long enough to scourge and purge the world around her. Trial by fire. Every time, every time: the end of everything. The Chimaera breathes her fire. She can't help it. The scorched trees. The charred stalks that were once living people. The sooty buildings and the smoke and.

Nothing makes sense. The world's alive. Nothing's happened, right? You're here and safe. The trees, the people, and the buildings are clean. There's no smoke.

It's inside me, all the trouble. But it feels like the end of everything I've known. I have to ask myself, what have I destroyed this time? It seems as if the world's gone through total fire. No life, no humanity, no love, nothing.

We were walking again, at once slower and faster. I felt we were accelerating toward something, but moving more patiently.

It takes a little while for my eyes to adjust, Q. At some point I realize I haven't destroyed anything, not anything real at least. But I'm scared something invisible has been lost. I have to think I've ruined something because I feel like something in me has been ruined. Every time my Chimaera arrives, I—.

A part of me dies in every fire. Burned up.

Every transformation subtracts. Every transformation wounds. Every transformation is a cause for grief. This is what I sensed then and know now for sure.

The monster inside the girl and inseparable: frightening and necessary and gruesome and simple-hearted, unreasonable but always in the right. The monster who can show up in the street or behind the steering wheel of a car traveling a winding two-lane road at sixty mph.

I knew I would love the Chimaera just as I loved Nest. They are each other, and they are one. I knew the Chimaera wanted and needed from me what Nest wanted and needed. Someone honest and patient, quiet, and brave enough not to run. A witness.

My father.

When the Minotaur falls asleep and my dad comes home, I know what he goes through. My mom always has to pick up the pieces of my father, and I'm not sure what that means for her. We've never talked about it. What would it mean for you to pick me up?

It might be worse for you, since I'm sure I'll need—.

I'm only going to get sicker.

In the aftermath, we'll sit or walk or hold each other, and one day, you'll be left with my body. Chimaera dead, and me.

I shook my head. But she was right, of course. Today, tomorrow, the day after, maybe she won't wake up, the Chimaera and the girl both gone.

We'll see.

But this has worked out. Today. Right now. You're walking with me still. We haven't been destroyed.

I don't know what I would've done.

You're brilliant, Q. All that light shining out of you.

■ ■ ■

Nest laughed. The Chimaera had come and gone, and we were in the heart of the city. Nothing had died or been lost. We walked.

Then, Nest found a story.

Money's a great motivator. In 1809, a Scottish gentleman named Robert Barclay Allardice walked a thousand miles in a thousand hours for a thousand guineas. Guineas were gold coins that were worth a little more than—it doesn't matter. They were solid gold coins, and, if he won, Barclay would run his fingers through piles of them. The original bet for a thousand guineas only started the pot. Captain Barclay, as he was known, took bets adding up to a hundred thousand pounds. He might've lost a huge fortune. He didn't. Every hour of every day for forty-two days, the captain walked a mile. All the way to a thousand.

No one should have bet against him. Barclay was famous for walking. One time, he walked seventy-two miles between breakfast and dinner. Another time, he walked sixty-four miles in ten hours. If there had been an Olympics then, he might have won for walking.

What's funny is that the captain walked the same mile a thousand times, more or less around the block. Nuts. He lost a lot of weight, thirty pounds, and barely slept, and.

In today's money, Barclay won nine million dollars.

■ ■ ■

The first person to walk around the world. Well, who knows? But the first person officially judged to walk around the world was from Minnesota. This is excellent trivia. Dave Kunst walked 14,452 miles over four continents. He had to take a couple planes to get over oceans, but that didn't count against him. If he could walk on water, he would be remembered for a lot more than strolling across continents.

The Soviet Union wouldn't let Kunst walk in Soviet territory. Cold War stupidity. Maybe the Russians sent out some poor guy to walk from Belgrade to Kamchatka, and from one end of Cuba to the other. I don't know, but that wouldn't have added up to 14,452.

Here's the thing: Dave Kunst didn't start his walk alone.

In June 1970, Mr. K started the walk with his brother John and a mule named Willie Makeit. Who else was going to carry their gear? Though I think they should've gone with a camel. No one thought of it, I guess. One mule later, violence. Way over in Afghanistan, thieves shot and killed John and wounded Dave. Much worse than a car driving over the curb. Dave recovered and began walking again from the spot where one brother was shot dead with his second brother, Pete.

At the end of mainland Asia, Dave sent Pete home and took on Australia alone. A third mule died, probably somewhere really inhospitable, like the burning desert. Again, I'm thinking: camel. But if Dave had had a camel, he might never have met his wife. Once the mule dropped dead, Mr. K had to drag along his supplies by himself, until a woman named Jenni Samuel, a teacher from Perth, Australia, caught up to him. Jenni offered to drive alongside the rest of the way, towing Dave's things for him, saving him. Of course he married her.

■ ■ ■

There's a reason we go to a high school for nerds: we passed the entrance exam. Enough said. I know you do, but I try not to think in math. Sometimes, though, I can't help it.

By the time he stopped in October 1974, four years after he started, Dave Kunst had gone through more than twenty pairs of shoes and walked more than twenty million steps. So, a pair of shoes might last a million steps. Give or take.

This is good math. Maybe even fun.

If I think, a yard per Nest step, three feet; 5,280 feet in a mile divided by three—.

Hold on.

— . . . —

One thousand seven hundred sixty steps per mile. Then a million steps divided by that. Easier to add zeroes and multiply.

— . . . —

Add two zeroes: 176,000, which is almost 200,000. Times five, a million; but—.

— . . . —

Really, Q, you look like you're hurting. I'm going as fast as I can.

A hundred seventy-six thousand goes into a million more than five times, but less than six. But we're talking about steps, and we added two zeroes, so—.

Let's say a million steps, rounding up, is around 600 miles. One pair of shoes to walk from—I don't know—Boston to Pittsburgh? Tel Aviv to, I'm guessing, Baghdad, not counting rough roads? Beijing to Seoul, walking on water? Copenhagen to Paris? That would make for something like four pairs of shoes to get you from Disney World to Disneyland.

And to make it personal—since it's all about me, after all—I estimate, today, I've already taken—.

Fourteen thousand steps.

And we're not even halfway.

■ ■ ■

I sometimes think about walking a long, long way. Across the country, ocean to ocean, or from here to Uruguay or

Labrador. Even if no one's done exactly that before, people have done all sorts of things like it, or in parts. Think of all the adventures thought to be impossible made possible. Think of everything men and women have survived.

"You'll be bothered from time to time by storms, fog, snow. When you are, think of those who went through it before you, and say to yourself, 'What they could do, I can do.'"

That's the kind of thinking that will keep you alive, or keep you hopeful. Or comfort you when your toes are black and bleeding. Or when the glare and heat of the sun turn your eyes to glass. Or when your mule dies.

MILE NINE

Something else that keeps you alive is food.

I won't lie. I was hungry. I needed

Fuel.

I promise, Q, we'll eat soon. You're a big boy, and.

Your cannoli was forever ago.

Here, take this. It's not much, just Life Savers. Have
the rest. You like Wint O Green?

And we'll get a couple bananas.

I usually don't eat much on these walks. I think and

think, watch and learn, and I forget. Finally, my body shouts over my brain. Then it's blueberries and water, or a peach, or grapes, or chocolate. Sometimes, if I have to, I get a sandwich, maybe *banh mi*, sometimes streetmeat, or a pretzel, or roast chestnuts. Or.

It's almost enough for my mind to eat itself. Thinking nearly gets me from one end of the walk to the other. But the body has its needs.

Fuel.

■ ■ ■

When I was young, my mom would make me hot bananas, sliced up, with milk and brown sugar. Actually, she still does, like a couple days ago, when I couldn't sleep. I can never be my mother, nothing as good, but I want to give comfort. To my friends, my children, strangers, you. How can anything be wrong with that?

I'm not sure what's more important to remember than to comfort another human being. This is the second part of hospitality, right? After making sure your guest has enough food and water, and a chance to heal from any wounds or sickness, then you give comfort to get rid of fear. You give sleep. You give bananas and milk and sugar. You give toast and butter, chocolate and quiet.

Hospitality might die with my mother. That's what my father says.

Mom will bring a sandwich and a glass of water to the man who repairs the boiler: whether or not he eats or drinks doesn't matter. Rain or shine, summer or winter, she invites the door-to-door canvasser inside for a rest and a glass of something. She buys the next-door neighbors, both sides, Christmas gifts. Maybe that's generosity, neighborliness, not exactly hospitality, but it's related. It's about stretching your care past your own walls.

"Martha," my father says, "you're the last of your kind."

"I hope not," my mother says.

Hospitality might die with my mother if my mother outlives me. But I want to carry it forward. If I live, if I keep my mind, I want to be hospitable.

Make a note to self, Q. For our future.

Always have a bed made. Keep extra bananas, milk, and brown sugar. Bread and meat. And maybe a pie.

■ ▦ ▨

What's worse for a mother than outliving a child?

If you die before your mother, Q—? It won't matter what kills you, will it?

It might matter, since the intolerable at least seems tolerable if what happens couldn't be avoided. I mean, if you die from an inoperable brain tumor or get struck by lightning, that brings out one kind of grief. But if a cop crushes your throat, and all you had in your pockets added up to cigarettes and a lighter; and your house keys; and a couple quarters, six dimes, two pennies, and your lucky rabbit's foot; and. That's different, right?

That grief is different.

Absolutely, but. Whether it's cancer or a chokehold, train wreck or suicide, sense or nonsense, doesn't change the one, true fact: a mother wants to die before her child. That's what they call the natural order of things, unless.

Unless you live to a hundred, like I will—then you might bury your children. If you live long enough, you'll bury everyone and everything: your parents; your friends; all your pets, except your last, tiny Chihuahua that barks night and day over your dead body; your children, your favorite and your least favorite; your husband or wife, and all the other half-loves, all the quarter-loves, all of them; and your full enemies. You can bury the truth about your life, whatever stories you choose, the most embarrassing stories, the worst stories, when you did this terrible thing, or gossiped, or drove someone else to their death; you can bury your teeth and hair and happiness. You'll bury everything except yourself.

If I die before my mom and dad, I hope my Chimaera kills me, roasts me dead. It might be a comfort for my parents to say to themselves, "It couldn't be helped. Beasts like that kill—."

■ ■ ■

Wow.

How did I get there from bananas and milk?

All I know is my mother has had reasons, I guess, to comfort me my whole life. I've always had things going on in me, always ideas and upset, always dreams.

When I was ten, fifth grade, I pretended hard enough to believe I had different-colored eyes. One amber, one violet. I could see Good through the amber eye and Evil through the violet. When both were open, I saw the real world, normal shadow, normal light, color, but I had no real idea of what to fear or trust. Only when I looked at the world one eye at a time, amber and purple, could I find Good and Evil.

159

I would close one eye, then the other, back and forth, to gauge the world. The good people, the good animals, the good spirits would shine, wrapped in gold, painted in gold. The evil: horizon-purple, night-purple; the heads of the wicked faced backward.

The shining Minotaur. My homeroom teacher dark, though, and frowning at the wall behind him. Our puppy, Julius, a golden Rottweiler; but our neighbor's toy poodle, deep purple, and her head turned one hundred eighty degrees. Crows purple, and their beaks the wrong way; the gold swallows. Gold trees, purple trees, depending on the spirits and gods under the bark, among the branches.

Amber moon, violet sun, and vice versa, depending. Dr. M like noon. And my parents? A thousand candles, the gold light too much, too painful.

I don't know. Maybe I went like this a year, until I met Akira with her violet eye and her amber eye. I couldn't believe it, and I asked her, "What do you see with your yellow eye? And what do you see with your purple?"

"I can see ghosts with the yellow eye," she said.

"Really?" I said.

"All the time," she said. "They're everywhere."

"Ghosts? I never see ghosts with my yellow eye. I only see what's good."

"You don't have a yellow eye," she said. "Both your eyes are—"

"I have eyes like yours. I can see Good and Evil."

"No one has eyes like mine."

She was right. No one has eyes like hers, and I felt afraid, defenseless.

"Ghosts?" I said. "For real?"

Akira nodded: "Everywhere."

▪ ▪ ▪

Did you see Akira's selfies from her grandmother's funeral? She posted them. All nine. At first, I thought, *This isn't right. Pretty tasteless.*

But Akira's too smart to—.

The pictures tell a never-ending story. The ninth almost duplicates the first and starts the story all over again, an endless circle. Beauty and sadness and.

Number one: Big smile, black dress, amber eye, violet eye, gorgeous; altar and pews; and you can see her grandmother's coffin over her shoulder, small, distant, almost out of range.

Number two: Flower arrangements, and Akira's standing over the lilies; the edge of the casket behind her, maybe the handle? A brass handle? You're not really sure.

Number three: Cross-eyed, and her mother in profile—black gloves, pillbox hat and veil—holding a tissue up to her nose. She has no idea what Akira's up to.

Number four: Open casket, milky satin and walnut; her grandmother's folded hands, cross and rosary, chin, nostrils, lace at her throat; Akira's right eye, the violet eye, and her forehead.

Number five: Akira crying.

Number six: Akira and her big brother. You can only see James's blue shirt collar and the start of his charcoal suit, the nap of his hair, his earlobe; Akira's eyes shut, and the rest of her face hidden in her brother's shoulder.

Number seven: Akira crying harder. Makeup sliding.

Number eight: Akira and the floating casket; pall-bearers.

Number nine: Big smile, black dress, Akira's face all stained with makeup. Purple eye, amber eye. You realize she's in the exact same position as number one: the church aisle, the pews and faraway altar. One big difference: no casket. Grandma's gone.

I texted Akira after I saw the nine pictures: Did you see any ghosts with your yellow eye?

Akira: ?

Me: Remember? You told me when we met you could see ghosts with your yellow eye.

Akira: I forgot. Let me look.

Me: Where are you?

Akira: Home. Hold on.

Me: Holding.

Akira: My grandmother's sitting at the end of the dining room table.

Me: How does she look?

Akira: Like herself. Happy. But now I'm crying.

Akira brought the nine selfies printed on one sheet to class. We're in that weird philosophy elective: Birth, Death, and Recurrence. We were talking about Jung and alchemy, and I don't know what. The ouroboros: the symbol of the serpent eating its tail. Endless birth, death, and rebirth; the balance between life and death.

Intense.

The amazing thing about picture nine is that Akira looks old. Ancient and dying. Not really, but. You could see what she might look like in sixty years. Akira will grow old and lie in a coffin. We will all lie in a coffin. You. Me. Some sooner than others.

In picture one, the casket was tiny and far away: as far from us as death. We never want to think about dying. But in picture nine, death seems close. Death has started to take over Akira's face. It only looks that way, though. How exhausting to cry over someone.

Do you see what I'm saying?

—?—

The selfies weren't stupid and obnoxious. They were about grief.

■ ■ ■

It might be a little late to ask, but do I talk too much? In general. I know I've been talking this whole time, but do I ever stop talking? Ever?

What if—?

What if you could only ever say one word, what would you choose? What would I choose? *Yes? No?*

I'd rather be more positive than negative.

But is *yes* the best I could do? How about *love*? If I could only ever say one word, it should be *love*.

Love would always stand for itself. It would never mean *cat* or *mat* or *bat* or any word other than itself. When I must sleep, I would not say, "Love love love." *Love* for every word, repeated over and over—? Worse than stupid, it would make love, the idea of love, meaningless.

No, *love* would always mean love.

What if *love*'s the only word I could say, and I could only say it a certain number of times? A hundred times or less. I would have to be careful with it. We are never careful with the number of words we use, are we? I would have to be careful with *love*.

For instance, you, because you're nice, ask, "May I buy you lunch at the Astro?" I would have to say, "Love."

Wait—: lunch? That's not important enough, is it, if I can only say *love* fifty times in my life?

Six *love*s, three each, when my parents die. Two *love*s for Julius. One now and then for nature, and maybe even one for this city—at night, the skyline and all the lights, while we're standing on the bridge. One occasionally for music or a play, but I can't imagine ever wasting a *love* on a movie or a television show, or on food, no matter how delicious.

You would get most of them, I think. If I ever find you crumpled up on the floor bleeding or crumpled up and crying, I'll say, "Love." Maybe I'll have to say *love* five or six times, close together, to bring you back.

When you're very old, and we've had a life together, and I never went completely and forever insane, just a few times for a week or two, and we raised a daughter, and I knew you were about to give everything up and die, I would stand next to you, and—even if it were my last one, and I knew I could never speak again, my only last word—I would say, "Love."

You know I would.

But what if, right now, while talking about this, on this walk, I use up the rest of my *love*s without knowing it—?

I'm so ridiculous. If I live a thousand years and want to say *love* with every breath, I would never run out. At the end, I would weigh as much as dust, and that one word would be half my weight, and.

I would die with a whisper: "Love."

■ ■ ■

One question anyone who's sane ends up asking, or maybe should ask, is, How cruel a master is insanity? How cruel is depression or schizophrenia or bipolar disorder?

I was hungry, and Nest was hungry, but some force kept her, and us, from sitting down for a meal, from buying a hot dog on the street or a pretzel. From resting and drinking water. Nest's mind kept us hungry, kept us from water, our lips dry, too dry.

Mania, which is one half of bipolar, and insanity grind on relentlessly. They make mercy nearly impossible. Like the cruelest slave driver, one who does not recognize humanity or allow for any recovery, insanity keeps the whip, cracks the whip, never drops the whip.

Yes, I was hungry, but I felt sorrier for Nest. I thought about all the times she wouldn't eat, hasn't eaten, enslaved, walking until she felt only strong enough to collapse.

But for me, Nest wanted to stop. For me, not for herself. At some point we would stop, I figured. She would find a way to rest for me, to get me to sit with her, to find

Fuel.

I have sympathetic hunger, I think. I know you're hungry, Q, so I'm hungry.

Soon.

Here's a sentence to chew on, a little snack after the banana. And I quote:

"Buffalo buffalo Buffalo buffalo buffalo buffalo Buffalo buffalo."

—?—

It's totally correct. Take all the time you need.

■ ■ ■

You know where we are? Irish Town. The art galleries and fancy little restaurants and money, all of this was slum and gangland. Irish Town is where you went if you wanted to get murdered. Criminals with names like Ears McGann and Darling Irene. Luke "the Barber" O'Casey killed between thirty and eighty people, maybe a hundred, until a mob lynched him from a lamppost. He really was a barber, but he was also a hit man, a police informer, and a vicious drunk, and he carried a very, very sharp straight razor. O'Casey killed people on the street, day or night. Swish: he'd open arteries in the throat or thigh. That light, fast razor: swish. His victims died before they hit the ground and bled into gutters. Before anyone knew what happened, the Barber would disappear into doorways, alleys, horse-drawn cabs, barrels and buckets, who knows? He'd be found in his parlor, a towel over his shoulder, razor in his hand, at a throat, shaving a man, steady. And the men in his shop would swear he'd never left.

Irish Town was leveled in 1947. Plowed under. Mayor Byrne had actually been born and raised here, one of eleven kids, and nothing made him happier than destroying the whole neighborhood, wiping it away. All the blood and crime and poverty. And here we are, nothing to worry about, strolling by really high-priced pottery and paintings and sequins and mannequins and plates of rabbit and penguin—do the rich eat penguin?—and shark and cheese, the best cheese.

I think every city has an Irish Town. Not all of them get destroyed or improved, and they're terrible. Right now, they're terrible. But how many cities have theaters where there used to be slave markets, and malls built on the sites of massacres?

The lost graves.

It's impossible to remember everything. A city builds on top of itself. Every so often, though, a memory gets discovered, a secret found. A bone, a skull, a shard, an arrowhead, a spoon, a torn-up doll. A story comes undone, a ragged end. Something great we'd forgotten, or something terrible we wish we never had to think about ever again. What's dead doesn't always stay dead.

■ ■ ■

In the middle of the Roman Forum, there's a stone called the *Umbilicus Urbis Romae*. The distances to and from ancient Rome were measured against it. Everything began and ended at the navel of the capital, the center of the empire, its belly button, the omphalos. Nothing is measured against it now.

Our city had its own navel, its own omphalos. We learn about Hake's Oak in elementary school. How many men and women were hanged from the branches? Twenty-seven, right? Four redcoats, five traitors, six murderers, seven cowards, three black boys, one woman, and a rapist. That's city myth, and everyone knows it. But only God knows how many people swung from Hake's Oak.

Before it was called Hake's Oak, it was Satan's Oak. And only the Devil knows how many people he screwed to the trunk.

That tree survived lightning, hurricanes, blizzards, cold, car wrecks, one bus, the hundred hands of God, and.

Every myth figured that tree would live forever. That it had human blood for sap. Or liquid iron.

How many fires were set at the roots? How many men went at it with saws and axes?

Then, the tree at our center died.

■ ■ ■

Our city stands at a crossroads. The crossroads might have been the intersection of deer paths, or where bears broke through the forest, or tribes traded goods. All of it. At the crossroads, there was a tree, thirteen feet wide, forty-some feet around, and, according to every memory, always old, always dark, and always huge. It became the witness tree for a real estate deal between the Devil and two trappers named Hake and Surridge. The Devil and the men each marked the tree, the Devil with his finger-nail, and the men with knives. The men gave up their souls, for sure, but each gave up a hand, too. Hake his right, and Surridge his left. Satan screwed their hands to the tree. There the hands stayed for fifty years. Until the Devil took them back.

Out of that deal between Satan and the trappers came the trading outpost that grew into the village that grew into the town that grew into this city. For two hundred years, Satan's Oak marked the center, the *umbilicus urbis*, of where we live. Finally—hear my sarcasm? Finally, the council ordered it cut down to make way for the new city hall. The witness tree died.

How long did it take to saw down that oak?

People protested. Even the vice president of the United States wrote a letter urging the mayor and council to allow "that steady witness to a part of the history of this great Union" to live undisturbed and even protected until it died a natural death, "as all living things must, in their time, die."

It didn't matter. Progress.

People wanted to chain themselves to the trunk, but no one had a chain long enough.

People wept.

How long to cut down that oak?

■ ■ ■

There's a wall plaque and a few photographs in the lobby of city hall, honoring Hake's Oak. You might make out the three scars, the Devil's scratch and the marks of Hake and Surridge. Some have claimed to see the branches sway and the leaves shake in the photographs.

Some have made out the shadows of hands in the bark.

After it was cut down, the witness tree was made into sawdust for the slaughterhouse floor, to soak up blood.

■ ■ ■

I keep coming back to death. I have to stop.

My Chimaera usually makes me sad, so—.

Maybe it's because I feel so close to life, walking with you. Or maybe it's because I've been hungry all along, so hungry.

Or maybe it's because we've been walking uphill, and I feel like I'm going to die.

We're getting to the steepest street in the city, at a grade of fourteen degrees and seventeen hundred feet above sea level. Don't worry, it only lasts a couple blocks, then down, down, down.

If you were a gentleman, you'd carry me.

No more talking. My heart's—

■ ■ ■

Don't you play football? Stop breathing so hard and look at the river.

Strange snake. No head, no tail: a mirror made of muscle.

Ess after ess after ess.

And way, way out, that purple-black ribbon is the ocean.

■ ■ ■ ■ ■ ■

Down, down, down we went. Tired, hungry.

Fuel.

We must have passed six, seven places to eat, reasonable places. If Nest couldn't stop, if her mind simply couldn't let her stop, I would have to force her to stop. I, the one with his mind and heart composed, would finally have to put my hand on Nest's shoulder and say, be bold enough to say, "It's time for us to eat. It's time to rest."

I think it's difficult to remember when you're around someone as powerful and smart and interesting as Nest, who also happens to have a difficult mind, that you are the more powerful. It seems the opposite. We don't seem to think as fast and as deep. We are not oceans; we are puddles. Or so we think.

But Nest's power comes from a frailty. Her power comes from a mind that could break itself. This is what it means to have a treacherous mind, to get sick from thought.

We might get hungry or tired, but our minds won't turn against us. We won't be killed by thoughts. We have no Minotaur, no Chimaera. But we have our needs, too, right? At some point we lose patience, or we can feel ourselves giving up. Until, at last, there's a spot of relief.

"And here we are," Nest said. "The Astro."

I think they renamed it after a renovation for the elderly pinball machine out back. When was the last time you played pinball? Ever?

I recommend the milk shakes and egg salad. And the pie. And the caramel crunch cake.

Do you like corned-beef hash?

Not here you don't.

▪ ▪ ▪

A waitress seated us at a booth halfway down the wall. The diner was busy but not packed: not quite lunchtime.

Q, would you trust me to order for you? I'm waiting for your voice. A little while more. Would that be all right—?

Look. You have to look. There's a terrible man. He eats like a jackal. Tearing at his food. Why can't he eat like a man? Scraps falling out of his mouth with every bite; chomping, bolting, talking, and. His wife's the little white-haired monkey across from him. Doesn't she move like a monkey, her fast mouth, faster fingers, and her eyes back and forth, back and forth, up and down? Her eyes anywhere but on her husband.

They have to be married. How long has the monkey hated sitting across from the jackal? If she sat next to him—. If she sits on his shoulder and eats her fruit and cottage cheese, picks at nits, then she doesn't have to watch him.

The jackal's talking and talking. His food's landing in his lap, on his arms, down his front, on his monkey-wife's plate—.

Maybe the jackal and the monkey have been married for fifty years. Maybe they'll die a week apart, one from old age, the other from a worn-out heart.

My parents have been married twenty years. Vladimir and Martha will love each other until the end of the world, long after death. Even if, one day, my father never returns from the labyrinth. Even if my mother drifts endlessly Between, not asleep, not awake, dancing with a cowboy.

■ ■ ■

The waitress brought us water and flipped to a clean sheet in a pad.

Nest ordered wheat toast and a vanilla shake for herself. Really? *I nearly said it.* What kind of lunch is that after all the miles? *I worried she'd order me a plate of cottage cheese and call it good.*

"He has laryngitis," *Nest said,* "but my friend here will have chicken soup, an egg salad sandwich on rye, fries, and three sides: bacon, sausage, and applesauce. And a chocolate shake."

Thank God. Nest did all right, though I might have gotten myself a plate of roast beef.

We waited for our food.

We waited a year.

You could go play pinball, or—?

Do you have favorite words, Q? Words that come easily to you? Like, *hut-hut-hike? Muscle, fist,* and *pencil? Rock, blood, ball?* Such a boy.

How about *cataclysm, murmuration,* and *quixotic?*

Titmouse, kitten, and *pony? Calculus?*

No—?

I have favorite words, Q. And some of them are sexy.

Nest lowered her eyelids halfway and pouted:

Sexy is as sexy does—.

   Don't laugh. You'll ruin everything.

   Now I have to return to center.

Nest closed her eyes, and when she opened them, they had become dark, smoky mirrors. She bit her lip to gather blood, to bring it red: her swollen mouth.

   Eclipse.

         Tooth.

               Nibble.

                     Thread.

                           Finger.

                                 Bone.

What was Nest doing to me?

   Her tongue and teeth. Gaze and lashes.

   Her sigh. Her throat—.

   Could Nest actually make me forget all about food? Could she make me want her now more than a meal?

   The waitress appeared.

   "Perfect timing," Nest said.

■ ■ ■

My soup came cold, something I never told Nest. I was too hungry to care. Fuel. So we ate.

Hungry. Hungry for Nest. Hungry all over. Egg salad, fries, applesauce, bacon, sausage. Shake. Soup. All the miles behind us, and all the miles to come. I only wanted to eat and eat and—.

"You need a poem while you eat."

That's what Nest said. And then:

Sea Poppies

Amber husk
fluted with gold,
fruit on the sand
marked with a rich grain,

I have to interrupt to admit something, no lie: the soup, the cold soup, had gotten warmer.

treasure
spilled near the shrub-pines
to bleach on the boulders:

Warmer—

your stalk has caught root
among wet pebbles

I cooled a spoonful with my breath.

and drift flung by the sea
and grated shells
and split conch-shells.

*"Conch-shells," Nest said, and I blew across another spoonful
of soup.*

Beautiful, wide-spread,
fire upon leaf,
what meadow yields
so fragrant a leaf
as your bright leaf?

*I left the last bit of soup at the bottom of the bowl, too hot to
drink.*

MILE TEN

You're the middle of the day, Q. You're right now. And almost every worry is gone, asleep.

But—.

Nest and I were out on the street, fed and warm. Sun everywhere. The infinite city of bright stone, concrete, and glass. I felt like I could walk a thousand miles. Nest knew how to keep me close. She knew to feed me right when I couldn't bear it anymore, so I would be happy and ready for anything.

I had our backpack: the books, the Millennium Falcon *in a bottle, water, and Nest's flannel.*

"Do you love me enough to keep going?"

Nest sensed my surprise, and that I wanted to speak.

"Shh," Nest cautioned. "There's more to go before I let myself hear your voice."

Let herself—?

I hitched the backpack and nodded over my shoulder, west.

No, this way, Q. I'm taking us where we have to go.

■ ■ ■

A destination?

I didn't think Nest had a plan, and maybe she didn't start with a plan, but she found one. When did she get a solid idea in her head? When did she decide she had to take me someplace? We'd drifted from where we started.

Still, I trusted.

And I trusted her that night a little less than a week ago. When we started the drive, Nest had no plan, not so far as I knew. She'd wanted to talk, and I wouldn't say no. We hadn't seen each other in two months before that ride, two months she was housebound and had refused to talk to me, two months of her suffering. Depression, the other side of bipolar, when she's infinitely tired and near silent. When the Chimaera cries and moans—.

Could she have found a plan then, too, her first night out, while driving with me? Had she thought of a place where we had to go? Did she know the exact tree where she could collide with a good chance of killing us both?

I don't know. I don't remember being afraid, and I don't remember fighting for control of the wheel. I don't remember wrestling with the Chimaera. And who's to say I hadn't been persuaded the destination she had in mind wasn't exactly right and perfect? Two young lovers dying together? It's an old idea, tried and true, no matter how pointless.

It's day six, and Nest sleeps. I want her to wake. More than anything else, I want my Nest to wake and stand.

■ ■ ■

On that walk, three years ago, we were just becoming something. Nest came up with a plan, maybe it was only a few moments old, just over lunch, when she figured out how to make me want her and how to let herself want me.

We were headed somewhere.

It scares me just as much to think of how love survives as how it dies.

Yeah. This is one of those moments when I think my mind is older than I am. When I'm not exactly sure what I'm thinking or sure of its importance, or if it—.

Love lives on surprise. But what if we fail to surprise? Or we surprise the wrong way? Love can die fast.

Am I making any sense at all?

I want to surprise you. I'm taking you somewhere I've only ever seen from the outside. It's been closed and hidden and locked a long time. We're going to find our way in, and we're going to stand in the sun, and we're going to lie down, and.

■ ■ ■

Sometimes we get surprises that make us love more or harder because we're afraid.

For a few months, just after they were married, Vladimir lived apart from Martha. Not very long, and not a separation or anything like that, as if they'd woken up from their wedding and realized they'd made a terrible mistake. Research called my father west; physics. But Martha's Popp was dying. As the youngest, she felt she had to stay with him and help her mother. They agreed Vladimir should go on without Martha; she would join him as soon as possible.

One month, two months, three months. They phoned, they wrote, they made the best of it. Popp held on, and Vladimir worked and thought, and one night got into a terrible car accident.

I memorized the letter he wrote and sent the next morning.

The noise of it, Martha, as the car, downside up, all wrong, revolved on its roof.

Imagine an undertow that drags you down and rakes you across the bottom of the ocean. All the cruel sand against your cheek. The sand scours your head, strafes your ear. This is the steel of the car roof against the asphalt, grinding and grinding—the noise of it.

But the noise came after.

One of my headaches, and the pain spiked, as it does. You know. Fishhook in my eye. A hardworking demon sawing through my skull. Lightning under my tongue. No wonder I lost track of the road.

When the car drifted onto the shoulder, I jerked the wheel, but the guardrail was right there—. I hit at the exact angle to send the car upside down. Upside down again. And I think once more. Three times.

Silence. That weird, deep silence, when I could say to myself, with all the time in the world, Everything will end. I could say to myself, Now, now, now, now, now, when you and I have gotten to the truth, now that we're married, now, I'm going to die.

No Angers. No Minotaur. The labyrinth destroyed. Everything done.

I waited. I waited a century. At last, the noise came.

And then?

Then it all stopped. The car stopped.

I imagine my father, Q, back at his university apartment, sitting at his desk with a cigarette, since he smoked then, about four in the morning, pen and paper, and exhausted.

The sea lets you go. The waves move through and past you. You stand again, soaking wet, coughing, but alive. The spindrift, the salt, and the first thing you hear is a wheeling gull.

I'd survived, and I heard a gull, in this case the radio, hissing.

An ashtray and the long ash at the end of his cigarette. The skinny smoke.

My father survived an accident that should have killed him, and he's writing the only woman he'll ever love.

I smelled a burning. I thought, I'll be burned alive.

I tried my door. It was crushed and wouldn't budge. The door across, no luck. So I reached behind and pushed open the door diagonal from me and shimmied out on my back. I got to my feet and brushed myself off as if I were a superhero. Dusty clothes, glass in my hair, but otherwise unhurt.

Someone spoke, a man: "I expected blood all over the windshield."

Then, a second witness: "Anyone else in the car with you?"

No. Only me.

The first witness evaporated. The second: "You must know you're blessed. Unbelievably blessed."

Blessed? I turned to look at the car. One door all but sheared off, twisted frame; a second and third door crushed; wheels collapsed; the whole thing overturned; the windshield blown apart; the underbody torn up.

I walked farther away, the second witness at my side—"You see you're blessed, don't you?"—the sirens coming and coming, and I thought about you.

How would I get back to you without a car? How would I tell you we nearly lost everything?

■ ■ ■

My mother flew out to my father.

"I had to go," she told me. "I didn't know who was driving that car. Your father or the Minotaur? The Angers? I didn't want him alone. I didn't want—."

"You didn't want him to die without you," I said.

"Popp was going, but he had Dye. They had their love, which you never saw. I was afraid for Dad. I knew what I had to do."

"Why didn't Dad call you after the accident? Why wait?"

"He did. Not right after, but the next day. We didn't have cell phones then, sweetheart. I mean, people did, but we didn't. He wanted to write it out of him first. And then, in the aftermath, his Minotaur. He called when he could."

"You must have been out of your mind," I said, "when you heard."

"No one as deeply in love as we were and young ever expects to be interrupted or broken by anything or anyone, let alone death. We had the Angers to deal with, the

Minotaur, but a car accident, something so stupid as that?"

Popp died during the time my parents were gone, but they, my parents, made it through. They drove home in an old car new to them. They drove twenty-one hundred miles over six days in July, when my mother was very, very pregnant. They raced against me. I was ready to be born.

■ ■ ■

I'm not going back to death and dying. I swear.

Once, though, I asked my mom: "If Vladimir had died, you'd have remarried, right? Sometime?"

My mother was chopping celery or onions or sweet potatoes for soup, and she chopped awhile.

"The whole flight out to your father," she began, "after his car accident, I thought about this and that, returning to all sorts of memories and ideas and daydreams. Mostly, I admit, I was afraid the plane would crash. 'Wouldn't that be just perfect?' I said to myself. 'Vladimir survives an awful wreck only for me to go down in this plane.' I couldn't keep myself from worrying. And then I couldn't even decide what I wanted more, to get there alive or dead. Life is hard, love is hard, and in death, love is perfect."

My mother stopped there, and I finally said, "That in no way answers my question."

"Oh," she said. "Doesn't it?"

"No."

She said, "I think it does."

I couldn't get my mother to say any more. She referred me instead to a poem.

I'm walking fast. I can feel it. We're nearly there. Where everything ends and begins.

■ ■ ■

I had no problem keeping up, but Nest did walk fast, and she got quiet. She stopped talking altogether for a long time. But I could see her smiling.

"Another block, then around the corner."

Nest was nearly running.

"Come on, Q. We're going to church."

■ ■ ■

"There," Nest said, slowing down. "Church of the Redeemer."

A dead church, really, boarded up and scorched. I had

some vague memory it had burned a year or two before. Arson.

"Come with me around back."

The church looked like the worst of its onetime parishioners: splintered and full of holes, sick, shocked. That building would have coughed, if it could. It would have fallen over and moaned. Instead, it stood there, burnt, tired, and quiet.

This desperate neighborhood—.

"Watch the glass."

Weeds and chunks of stone; broken wood, plastic bags, and paper. Somewhere, the sound of birds.

"Here, Q. This is it."

Behind the church, there was an area surrounded by a dark fence about eight feet high. No Trespassing. Keep out.

"I don't see any holes," Nest said. "Pick me up."

It was nothing to boost Nest, and I pulled myself up after her. Over the fence and in.

■ ▦ ▩

I've wanted to see this place for a long time. Last spring, the two of us, my Chimaera and I, sat together outside the fence. I cried, and she breathed fire until she went to sleep. We never went inside.

We stood in a living garden. It might have been overgrown and every bit as neglected as the church, a dead garden, but it was alive.

When she left I could—.

The flowers, Q. They smelled so good, but I could also smell smoke and shit and garbage. I thought, *Where are all the flowers?* And I thought, *I'm crazy.*

I tried to look through the dark fence, to find some way over: I knew.

I knew: "I'm crazy, and I need this garden."

The ghostly flowers and trees, and a shadow on hands and knees in the corner.

October, and the wounded church had its back to the garden. It faced another way, and the garden breathed.

Someone works very hard. The gardener never rests. He or she prunes and clears and digs and sows and harvests and.

For the first time, Nest held my hand.

A Biblical Garden, Q. Plants from Scripture.

Hyssop.

Fig.

Sage.

The east/west path; the north/south path. The perimeter.

Broad beans and broom.

This is a place for slowness, Q.

Mint.

A place for patience.

Delphinium and heath.

Do you feel that—?

That's slowness.

The birds and thorns.

Meadow saffron, rue, and rose.

Slowness is not the same thing as waiting.

Saffron and more saffron.

Mustard, dandelions—.

Slowness can last forever, Q, but waiting ends.

Cedar.

Myrtle—.

Waiting ends.

Her kiss came at the intersection of paths. The center of the
garden and a surprise.

Thistle.

All the waiting ended here.

Mallow.

And the slowness began.

Almond.

■ ■ ■ ■ ■ ■ ■ ■ ■ ■ ■ ■

We kissed, and the sun was bright. We took our clothes off.
    Which one of us was smiling? Which one laughed?
    Slowness.
    No speed. And no Chimaera. No wildness or talk. No
Angers. Almost no fear.
    We weren't two seventeen-year-olds having sex, or making
love, or rutting like animals. Nest wasn't losing her virginity.
Don't call it that. Don't ever call it that. We were love.

We were love. Right there, in the dirt, in the middle of a garden, behind a burnt-out church.

The sun.

We were love. Everything else was sky.

Or maybe everything was earth—.

Hard to know.

But when we rested, we rested Between, not awake, not asleep, together.

Until Nest spoke.

■ ■ ■

HE BIDS HIS BELOVED BE AT PEACE

I hear the Shadowy Horses, their long manes
   a-shake,
Their hoofs heavy with tumult, their eyes
   glimmering white;
The North unfolds above them clinging,
   creeping night,
The East her hidden joy before the morning
   break,

The West weeps in pale dew and sighs passing
away,
The South is pouring down roses of crimson
fire:
O vanity of Sleep, Hope, Dream, endless
Desire,
The Horses of Disaster plunge in the heavy
clay:
Beloved, let your eyes half close, and your
heart beat
Over my heart, and your hair fall over my
breast,
Drowning love's lonely hour in deep twilight
of rest,
And hiding their tossing manes and their
tumultuous feet.

■ ■ ■

That's the poem by William Butler Yeats my mother
sent me to find. The poem to answer my stupid question,
whether or not she would have married again if my father
had died. It's my favorite poem. It's the poem you would

recite for me from memory, right now, if you could, if you knew it. We could say it together, for each other, two voices.

I want your voice, Q, while we're lying here in the path, in the light, in the middle of flowers and thorns and fruit and.

I want to sleep with you. Until we get cold and have to stand up and walk the ten miles home.

Why aren't we cold?

■ ■ ■

You're putting me to sleep, Q. I can feel it.

But I want to hear you say my name. Please.

Remember our slowness—.

My whole name. Beginning, middle, and end, like you believe in its story and everything I've said this morning.

The miles—.

All of them—.

Between again, and I could barely make out Nest's sleeptalk.

I want to hear you say my name, Q.

Slowly, name by name by name.

Eleanor.

Nest.

Fitzgerald.

But I have to sleep—.

Let me sleep a little while first. Like this. My head on your chest.

I won't sleep long. I promise. The sun will disappear, and we'll get cold, and.

I'll only dream once.

■ ■ ■

I don't remember what happened after Nest fell asleep. She must have woken up, but did we feel the cold? Did we miss the sun?

Did I ever speak her name?

Did we pick ourselves up off the ground and fix our clothes? Did we rob the garden, steal bitter herbs and saffron? Did we ever eat figs?

Did we make it over the fence and reenter the city?

Even if she let me talk, did I only listen?

Did we hold hands, mile after mile, until home? Or did I carry Nest the whole way?

If I carried her, I promise, I never once put her down.

For Michèle